"As I was going to St Ives…"

Whitsun 1732

Mary Carter

Illustrations by Jan Biggs

"As I was going to St Ives..." Whitsun 1732

ISBN 0 9533940 1 8

Published by
Westmeare Publications
c/o The Norris Museum
St Ives
Huntingdon, Cambs PE27 4BX

First published in 2002

© Mary Carter 2002
Illustrations by Jan Biggs

All rights reserved. No part of this publication may be reproduced, stored in a retrieval system or transmitted in any form or by any means, mechanical, electronic, photocopying or otherwise, without the prior permission of the Publisher.

Publication of this volume has been made possible by a generous grant from the Goodliff Fund of the Huntingdonshire Local History Society

Other Publications by the Author
Edmind Pettis's Survey of St Ives, 1728, ed Mary Carter
Hemingford Grey is Famous for its Enormous Gooseberries – History through Road Names
"Town or Urban Society? St Ives in Huntingdonshire, 1630-1740" in Societies, Cultures and Kinship, 1580-1850, ed C Phythian-Adams
Not an Easy Church – A History of the Free Church in St Ives, 1672-1981, (under the name of Mary Wagner)

— — — with seven wives.

Preface

In 1732 Whit Sunday fell on the 28th of May. It was a busy week for St Ives in Huntingdonshire. Holy Communion was celebrated on that day, the Whitsun Fair took place on Monday and on Tuesday twelve children threw dice on the altar to see who could win six Bibles. During the week the parson baptised Mary Simpson, Edward Whiteside and Elizabeth Townsend, married John Steel to Elizabeth Burket and buried the daughter of John Knightley. These were routine events in the life of the town. But also in that year an elderly man called Edmund Pettis copied a list of names into the pages of his note-book. He had started his book four years earlier and was writing down what interested him about the town. This little leather bound volume gives us information about St Ives unobtainable elsewhere.

St Ives was a small town whose Monday market was well known for the sale of cattle and sheep. It lay six miles from the county town of Huntingdon and twelve from the university town of Cambridge. It benefited from trade on the river Ouse between Kings Lynn and Bedford and road traffic between London, Ramsey and Kings Lynn. Its population was about 1700. Apart from many inns, the only public buildings were the parish church and the three nonconformist meeting houses belonging to the Presbyterians, Baptists and Quakers.

Each wife had seven sacks.

'As I was going to St Ives: Whitsun 1732' is based on information given in the survey of Edmund Pettis supplemented with local material and with general information on daily life in the early eighteenth century. It is a description of St Ives through the eyes of a visitor called Jeremiah Horner. His visit has been used to recreate the life of the town and its inhabitants. Although I have invented his movements all other details are based on research. Contemporary quotations are printed in italics and sources are listed at the end of the book.

My special thanks are due to Jan Biggs for her delightful illustrations, Esther Newbold for photographs, Stewart Denham for plans and technical assistance and Bob Burn-Murdoch for so much encouragement over the years that it cannot be itemised. Illustrations from the Pettis' Survey of St Ives, of Cromwell's barn and the Salutation Inn are by courtesy of the Norris Museum, St Ives.

Each sack had seven cats.

Jeremiah Horner

Jeremiah Horner has been chosen as the central character because his family is well documented. His parents married in 1683 and he was born two years later, the oldest of six children. His mother died when he was young. When he was fourteen his father married Mary Cooper a widow. In the next year his father rented sixty acres of farmland in St Ives and in 1710 he acquired the Unicorn inn. He went to Huntingdon in 1691 with two others to obtain a licence for a Presbyterian meeting house in St Ives. His family's connection with this church survived into the middle of the nineteenth century. When he died in 1720 he left everything to his second wife with specific bequests to his children. His son Robert was given his best clothes and his gold ring, John his grey suit and Joseph 'the suit I now wear'. Jeremiah and his sister Susanna received silver and Mary, another married daughter, linen.

Jeremiah was a butcher in Whitechapel in London. Children started work very young in the eighteenth century. Daniel Defoe said of Norfolk 'that the very children after four or five years of age could everyone earn their own bread'. In St Ives apprenticeships of paupers started at about fourteen. The sons of 'the middling sort' like Jeremiah expected to leave home at the age of sixteen or seventeen. We do not know why he chose a different trade from his father. I have assumed that

Each cat had seven kits.

he served an apprenticeship. If so, he was lucky that his father could afford to pay the necessary premium. This might have cost him £10 when his annual income was probably less than £100 per annum. His overwhelming concern would be to ensure that his son entered a trade that would enable him to support himself. After his apprenticeship, Jeremiah would need capital to set himself up as a master butcher and to marry. Those without access to capital worked as journeymen, day labourers or paid employees.

Why did Jeremiah leave St Ives? Was it the arrival of a stepmother or the natural desire of a young man to see London? The capital city was certainly a magnet. It has been estimated that one in six of the entire population of England had been to London at some time. It was the largest city in Europe but also a very unhealthy place. One in three babies died before the age of two. Tuberculosis and smallpox were rampant. London constantly needed healthy newcomers to replace those who had died from disease.

Jeremiah lived to the east of the city in Whitechapel. London had already spread beyond the square mile, the area within the original Roman walls. Whitechapel had been important for the supply of food. During the seventeenth century the country lanes had become busy city streets. The main streets were laid out in a grid with handsome houses but behind lay small tenements and shacks called rookeries crowded into tiny alleys. They competed for space with industries like the manufacture

kits cats sacks and wives ~ ~

of cannon and glassware as well as a myriad of other crafts. It must have seemed like a world away from his home town of St Ives.

Jeremiah had married Ann Collier on the 29 September 1728 and might be bringing her to St Ives to visit the family. Possibly he was a widower as it would be unusual if he were marrying for the first time at the age of forty-three. She may also have been a widow. There were advantages in this. She could already have shown that she was a good mother and housewife. Men often married widows who were older than themselves, as marriage to an older woman would limit the possible size of a new family. At all events Jeremiah was following the example of his own father who had brought home a new wife to manage his home and care for his existing children.

In 1729 his stepmother had died leaving him the Unicorn Inn. £25.5s was left in bequests to the other children, her best clothes to Ann, Jeremiah's wife, and the rest of her clothes to her other daughters-in-law. As a widow his step-mother had clear legal rights to leave property as she saw fit, unlike married women who '*as soon as they are married are wholly at the will and disposition of the husband. They can own no goods, not even their clothes.*' We can imagine Jeremiah, now 47 years of age, deciding to visit the town. He had agreed to sell the Unicorn but the actual process of selling was very slow and he needed to visit the town to finalise the sale. He could also combine his trip home with business at the Whitsun Fair.

*"Seven Wives" drawings based on
an original idea by Bob Burn-Murdoch*

The Journey

Jeremiah and Ann had not made the decision to travel lightly, as the roads in England in the first half of the eighteenth century were atrocious. Even fifty years later a writer talks of the deep ruts full of water with hard dry ridges, which caused coaches to overturn. In winter the roads became a sea of mud and were frequently unusable. Wooden axles and wheels often broke and passengers could be thrown out and left to wait until help arrived. An old lady once yoked six oxen to go to church as her horses were unable to get through the mud. Another problem was the risk of attack by highwaymen. Even the Prime Minister was held up and robbed later in the century. Provided passengers surrendered their money, rings, watches and silk handkerchiefs quickly, highwaymen were generally described as polite, '*begging to be excused for being forced to rob, and leaving passengers the wherewithal to finish their journey.*' It was rare for waggons to be attacked as passengers in them had less to lose and the goods they carried were often bulky. The threat of robbery was seen as a direct result of the increasing wealth of the country.

There was more than one way to go to St Ives. Jeremiah could hire a horse and ride but a single horseman with a pillion passenger was at risk from footpads. A place in a stagecoach would ensure that they were treated with some respect. A stagecoach to Huntingdon left from the Red Lyon in Aldersgate Street on a Wednesday or Saturday. An inside seat was expensive. The windows were kept closed with board or leather curtains because the English did not like fresh air which they considered bad for their health. A passenger would be wedged in tightly between strangers, drunken, smelly or restless in a stuffy and dark coach. Alternatively he could sit on the top and endure the weather or dust. It was however difficult to sit on the top of a coach as passengers had to concentrate to keep their balance with only a small handle to help.

If they took the stagecoach as far as Huntingdon they would either have to get a carrier to take them the next six miles to St Ives or hire a horse or even walk. Alternatively they could ask to be set down where the road forked outside Papworth Everard and walk the remaining six miles to St Ives. But foot passengers were always looked on with suspicion as either footpads or beggars. Another option was to take a carrier to St Ives either from the Red Lion or the Three Cupps in Aldersgate, or the Red Lion without Bishopsgate Street. In the previous century Thomas Johnson had been a carrier from St Ives who visited the Cross Keys in White Cross Street on a Wednesday and returned on a Thursday. I have assumed that a similar service continued. As Jeremiah's sister had married a Johnson they would be travelling with a relative.

In good weather a carrier could make a maximum speed of four miles an hour. Measurements were taken from the Standard (a wooden post) in Corn Hill in the centre of London. Edmund Pettis on his map computed the journey from London to St Ives at 58 miles but this was not the same as post stage measurements. For example they claimed 42 miles to Caxton, while Pettis said it was 50. Weights, measures, the length of a mile, even the time of day varied regionally across the kingdom. It was the advent of stagecoaches and the railway that gradually led to the standardisation of time and distance across the country. Following Pettis's calculations the journey would take fifteen hours from London. However as a century later a carrier regularly left Godmanchester at seven and arrived the following day in Bishopsgate twenty-one hours later we can assume that the journey would take the best part of twenty four hours.

One imagines Jeremiah and Ann leaving home dressed in their best clothes. He may, like his father before him, have owned three sets of clothing. A good suit of clothes lasted at least fifty years and would be handed down to the next generation. But as a Londoner he would try to copy his betters and dress as fashionably as he could afford. Foreigners noticed that all classes wore the same kind of clothes, even if some were ragged and dirty. Although full bottomed wigs were still worn by the gentry, as a wealthy tradesman Jeremiah would possibly have a shorter style known as the tie wig which had the curls at the back held together with a black ribbon at the nape of the neck. It was pomaded and

powdered. His hair was cropped short under his wig. He would wear a coat with a full skirt that was left unbuttoned to show his long waistcoat buttoned to the waist. At his neck he tied a simple short neck-cloth. His breeches fitted his legs to just below the knee and were of the same dark fabric as his coat. Beneath them he wore a pair of linen drawers. A garter below the knee held up his woollen stockings and his shoes were square toed with a buckle. He took with him his great coat which was belted at the waist to protect him from the weather. He also had a three-cornered hat, leather gloves, cane and fob watch in his waistband pocket and a bag.

Ann would first put on a chemise and then tie a string round her waist from which two pockets hung, one on each hip. Her worstead stockings held up by garters were in white or black with coloured clocks. Sometimes women embroidered sayings on their garters, like *'My heart is fixt, I cannot range.'* She wore high-heeled shoes with pointed toes. If the streets were mucky she could put pattens or clogs over them for protection. Pattens were wooden overshoes on tall metal rings. Next she wore a set of stays which were metal or whalebone strips, sewn between layers of cloth. Her petticoat showed through the opening of her skirt. The skirt was very full to cover her side hoops and the bodice had sleeves fitted to below the elbow possibly with flounces or ruffles. To keep herself warm she had tucked a neckchief into her low cut dress. She also had a short cloak for warmth. Straw hats tied on top of a lace cap were popular. She wore her hair in the new fashion in a bun at the back of the head with curls around her face.

On Friday 3rd May I have made them walk before dawn the short distance from their home in Whitechapel to the Cross Keys to travel with the carrier from St Ives. I have made Jeremiah accompany the waggon on a hired horse while Ann rode in it. His family might have asked him to bring some luxuries that were cheaper in London. These could include powder sugar, rice, Poland starch, coffee berries, teas and unusual spices. Tea was so expensive that in 1722 the amount of tea consumed in a year amounted to one ounce per person. They might bring some lace trimming as a gift for the women in the family and tobacco for the men. Travellers expected to share the space with goods of various kinds. As it was coming up to Whitsun it is possible that the stage waggon was full of passengers and their goods to sell at the fair. If it rained the carrier might put up some kind of awning to provide shelter. The waggon was pulled by eight horses and the carrier sometimes rode and sometimes walked with the horses.

Their route took them north along Ermine Street (A10) to the turnpike at (Stoke) Newington and on to the toll-bar at Stanford Hill where Ann descended from the slow moving waggon to walk up the hill. Here she could see the gallows, perhaps with a corpse suspended from it. It was a popular English pastime to gather to see a hanging. The unfortunate man would be strung up from a cart on to the gallows. When the cart moved away he was left hanging by the neck. Relatives and friends would rush forward and pull on his legs to make sure that death came quickly. Others would touch the body because they believed it possessed magical powers. Even quite poor people clubbed together to purchase a penny account of the deaths of murderers and highwaymen.

The great northern post road to York was always busy. Defoe wrote of the *'excessive multitude of carriers and passengers, which are constantly passing ,,, with droves of cattle, provisions and manufactures*

for London.' It had '*tolerable good ways and hard ground till you reach Royston and to Kneesworth a mile farther. But from thence you enter upon the clays, beginning at the famous Arrington Lanes, and going on to Caxton and Huntington.*' Here the waggons left the roads deeply rutted and the frequent herds of livestock increased the problem. At least at this time of the year, they would not meet the large-slow moving flocks of geese being driven to London. They would see pedlars with their long string of packhorses carrying small goods for sale around the country. There were men, sometimes accompanied by the whole family, tramping along the roads. Such money as they had would be sewn into the lining of their coats as a precaution against footpads. '*We daily see manufacturers (artisans) leaving the places where wages are low and removing to others where they can get more money.*'

Travellers would meet postmen carrying letters to and from London. They rode very old horses and were frequently abused for being late in their deliveries or for taking shelter from the rain. There were also complaints about the cost of the post. Three pennies were charged within ten miles of the General Letter Office in London but more outside. At least St Ives now had a direct system of sending post to London. The post stage from March to St Ives to Caxton had started at the beginning of the

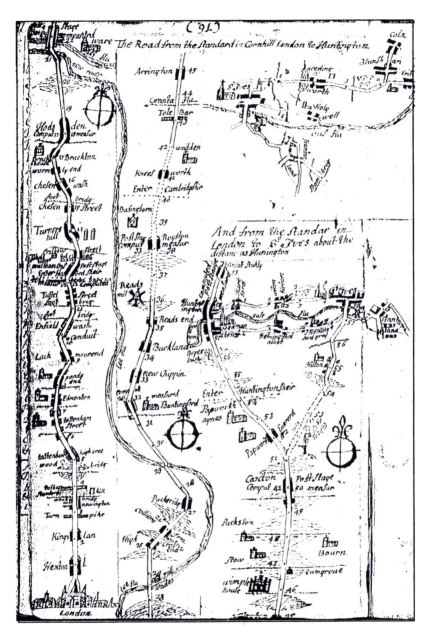

14 *Map of route from London to St Ives drawn by Edmund Pettis*

eighteenth century. Earlier letters had been carried on foot to Huntingdon and thence to London.

From Stanford Hill the road passed through Tottenham and Edmonton to the post stage and second toll-bar at Waltham Cross. By now they could notice the improvement in the air. London and other cities were surrounded by piles of filth and dung which produced obnoxious smells. So much coal was burnt that the air was frequently thick with smoke and dust. Their next stage ran through Cheshunt and Hoddersdon to Ware and from there through Buntingford to Royston. Here the road turned east to Cambridge or north on Ermine Street, the old Roman road, to Huntingdon. The first toll-bar on the road out of Royston was between Wadden and Arrington. At the Caxton post stage, there was a second gallows, which can still be seen. After Papworth Everard the road forked, the main route going to the Huntingdon post stage and the minor across open scrub land through the little village of Hilton to St Ives. This road was not tolled and was little better than a rough track. If the surface became too bad a cart would take to the open land to try and avoid the worst of the potholes. Dr Dale who visited the area at this time wrote that roads as such outside towns and villages often did not exist, nor even bridle-paths. He covered his journeys by riding across open country sometimes on more or less well-trodden paths. Their waggon took the better route to Godmanchester and then through the Hemingfords to St Ives. That way the waggoner expected the road surface to be passable.

It was the responsibility of the parish to keep the roads in its area in a good state of repair. The squire and the farmer were expected to send a number of horses, carts and people to provide six days' labour each year. Many parishes had converted labour to money but there was no real incentive to improve the roads apart from scraping away the mud at the end of each winter and throwing stones into the potholes. Turnpike trusts were being set up by the Government. They allowed groups of people to undertake to repair and maintain roads between specified places for a period of 21 years with the right to charge tolls on travellers. The trust between Royston and Wansford Bridge on the Great North Road in 1710 was one of the earliest but an amendment to the act in 1722 makes it clear that the surface of the road was still bad. New trustees were appointed and the road divided into three sections. As the section north of Huntingdon was in the worst state the first repairs were made there.

15

Jeremiah would have to suffer the potholes and ruts of the old surface on his stage.

Charges were levied at each stage. For the seven toll-bars between London and Papworth a coach paid the substantial sum of ten shillings and sixpence. As Jeremiah was riding his own horse he paid ten and a half pennies. Passengers were given a ticket which had its corner torn to show that it had been used. Charges were considered high and tolls unpopular. Those caught avoiding them were taken before a Justice of the Peace and fined twenty shillings, half of which went to the informer and the other half to the trustees for the roads. There were also attacks on turnpike gates and tollkeepers' houses.

We will imagine that Jeremiah and the other passengers avoided the worst of the dangers from an overturned waggon to an attack by highwaymen. Fifty-eight miles later they would without doubt have been tired and sore and longing for the end of their ordeal. As the waggon trundled down the last stretch, now called the London Road, they could at last see St Ives. Ahead of them was the medieval bridge with an inn to each side, a small building with smoking chimney on the bridge and the low roofs of the town behind. To their left, as the new day dawned, they might see the soaring spire of the parish church, a dominant feature in the landscape. As they came up to the bridge there were meadows on either side possibly still misty, countryside which Thomas Carlyle much later described as having '*a clammy look, clayey and boggy.*'

The first inns were the Dolphin on the left and the White Horse to the right. The Dolphin was of two storeys with attics and cellars. It had recently been rebuilt at great expense and was now a handsome brick building with sash windows on two floors and dormer windows in the roof. The windows in the frontage were regularly spaced with a central door opening on to the road. The hall was panelled as were two rooms on the first floor. The staircase had turned and fluted balusters much admired by those in the town. In 1718 the innkeeper had died unexpectedly. He had been out fishing. *'Being taken with a fit he had tumbled into the river and was drown'd.'*

Opposite was the White Horse. During the tedious journey fellow passengers might regale newcomers with stories of local murders. A gentleman called John Banson from Little Shelford near Cambridge was riding to St Ives '*over a place called the great Doles*' on Plough

All Saints Church seen from across the meadow

Monday, the twelfth of January, when the ploughing season traditionally commenced with festivities. Those working the fields told him that according to local custom there was a fine of one penny for anyone riding over the fields on that day. Banson objected and according to one version *'Offley did throw his cudgell which struck John Banson on the right side of his head, and uppon the blow he fell immediately from his horse dead for a while, and being taken up did bleed at the mouth and nose extremely and dyed about one of the clock the very next day.'*

Another murder had taken place at the White Horse. A certain John Hodgson had been pulled dead from the river in 1667. *'Fower or three years'* after his death a tailor from Swavesey called Edward Grime said that William Barton was his bedfellow at the White Horse. Sharing beds in an inn was quite common at this time. *'Hearing a great noise in the White Horse Inne, Grime did ask Barton when hee came to bedd unto him, what he did know since that this same day the said Hodgson was found in ye River and taken up with his head much beated, some of his teeth knocked out....Barton bade Grime hold his peace, for hee said hee did know how it cam.'* The innkeeper Thomas Bond, William Barton of Needingworth and John Nelson a victualler of Overcote were accused of murdering Hodgson. Grime's evidence amounted to little more than this and the three were acquitted, although one imagines that trade suffered for a while. In spite of such stories, these two inns were popular as travellers could leave their waggons and horses there and cross the bridge on foot to avoid paying a toll.

Before the bridge the carrier slowed down. The road here was low and liable to flood. The causeway lifting it above the water was not to be built until the nineteenth century. At a little brick building in one of the pedestrian refuges of the bridge the last toll was paid. The tollkeeper opened the gate to allow the waggon to cross the bridge. Tolls were collected by the estate of the Duke of Manchester who owned the rights to the bridge. Ann might marvel at the small house on the bridge with its little window where tolls used to be paid. When in 1540 Henry VIII had seized the great medieval abbey at Ramsey he also acquired much of St Ives including this chapel. He disposed of the chapel which was converted into a dwelling house with one room on the level of the bridge and a cellar below. It must have been pretty dilapidated because it was to be renovated in 1736 when two more storeys were added to the top of the building. Possibly the balcony to the cellar was also built at this time as a privy (toilet), draining into the river which also provided water for drinking and washing. But the bridge itself was in good order with a new cobbled surface and a brick parapet. During the Civil War in 1645 the Roundheads had destroyed the southern part of the bridge to impede the army of King Charles 1. The last two arches were removed and replaced by a drawbridge. The townsmen had to wait until 1716 before the duke rebuilt it with two new rounded arches and the parapet.

As the passengers reached the crest of the bridge they saw Bridge Street ahead with the Crown Inn facing them. (This is now Readwell's, the newsagents, and Woolworth's.) To their right they might be able to make out the Quay and perhaps the dark shapes of barges. Back from the water's edge the doors of more inns and private houses might still be locked up for the night. On their left was a good looking large timber building, now called the Manor House. The carrier urged his tired horses up Bridge Street, past the Cross and stopped outside the Salutation Inn next door to the Crown Inn. One can imagine the bustle and noise as the carrier halted his horses and the passengers jumped down to be greeted by family and friends. Jeremiah handed in his hired horse and walked with Ann past the Crown into the Bullock Market, (the Broadway), until he reached his old home, the Unicorn Inn.

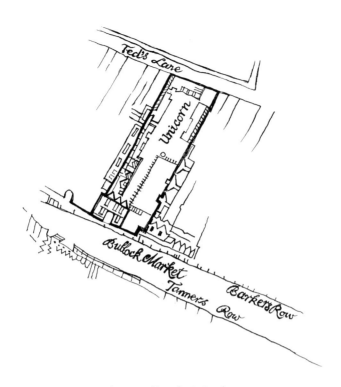

The Bullock Market

The Unicorn, was a medium-sized inn on the north side of the Bullock Market. It had two windows and a central doorway on the ground floor and three windows upstairs. There might have been attics. There was a row of four single storey buildings at right angles behind and a wide entrance. The yard was unusually large with stables, outbuildings and a back entrance from Ted's Lane now called West Street. After the fire in St Ives in 1689 some buildings were rebuilt in the new fashion in red brick with sash windows, but the Unicorn like many older buildings in the town was a timber framed building of wattle and daub. The roof would probably be thatched although tiles were made in St Ives. It is now Wadsworth's wine shop and the Constitutional Hall.

Travellers found the quality of English inns very variable. Some travellers talked of *'neat inns, well-dressed and clean people keeping them, good furniture and refreshing civility.'* But Arthur Young graded the inns he visited as *'bad'*, *'dirty'* or *'dear'*. Another traveller complained that he was obliged to share his room with a fellow-guest who was drunk. *'Right under this bedroom was a tap-room. The floor shook. Drinking songs were sung... I was hardly able to sleep with such a noise and bustle, and had just dozed off a little when my sleeping-partner arrived who knocked into my bed. With great difficulty he found his own and threw himself onto it just as he was – clothes, boots and all'*. Other problems might be flies, fleas and mice. A traveller once complained that he had found a rat gnawing his wig. However good or bad the service, tipping was expected. A maid or servant might only receive £3 a year in wages and any tips could double her income. She started her apprenticeship at fourteen and expected to receive free bed and board and cast-off clothing. Her leather stays, double quilted horsehair petticoat, stuff gown and linenshift would last for years. It was taken for granted that maid-servants were available for the men in the house. Cooks had an advantage in that they were allowed to sell dripping and cinders and if they did the shopping they expected to receive commission from shopkeepers. Live-in servants expected to eat well and some were adept at stealing. Their hours of duty were extremely long, generally from dawn to dusk, with hardly anytime for themselves.

Jeremiah's brother-in-law James Everitt was running the Unicorn until the sale was finalised. He had suffered the double blow of losing his wife, Jeremiah's sister, and his little daughter Elizabeth in 1728. There were two surviving children, Mary aged eight and Thomas aged five. Another daughter had only survived one year.

One imagines Jeremiah and Ann hoping to sleep for a few hours after the long and exhausting journey. Before going to sleep Jeremiah removed his wig and put on a nightcap, rather like a turban, and a nightgown. He and Ann shared a pot of posset. This drink was a blend of eggs, cream and sack or ale. It consisted of a frothy head of custard floating on a draught of highly alcoholic liquor. The custard was eaten with a spoon while the liquid was sucked piping hot through the spout of the posset pot which had been wrapped in cushions to keep it warm.

Their bed was a rectangular wooden frame that was quite short not because people were shorter but because they slept in a semi-sitting position propped on bolsters and pillows. The frame of the bed was laced from side to side with cord and a mat was spread on top. Beds, or as we

would say mattresses, were piled on top of the mat. The bed had both a flock and feather mattress. In grander houses there were so many mattresses that a set of steps was provided to climb on to the bed. The bed also had a bolster, one or two pillows, a sheet, blankets, coverlet and a rug. Rugs were used on the bed and not on the floor. Curtains around the bed provided privacy and kept out draughts, but more importantly if there was a canopy it provided protection. Many rooms were open to the eaves and there was generally a hole in the wall high up to allow the entry of birds or bats. An owl was welcomed as it could catch the rats and mice that came out at night. If his London house was more up to date, Jeremiah might have had a modern boarded ceiling. In the bedroom there was a small livery cupboard with a shelf with holes in the sides for ventilation. There was also a press-cupboard or wardrobe fitted with two doors and decorated with carving. There was a chamber pot and close stool to conceal it. Bedrooms were not solely used for sleeping and most in St Ives contained tables and chairs. A single curtain hung at the window.

On the first floor there were two other bedrooms. The two little children slept there with the maids. As a baby the boy had been dressed in swaddling clothes, with his arms and legs bound tight. It was thought that this made the body grow straight. As a toddler he wore frocks like his sister, with a petticoat, drawers or trousers underneath. He also wore a padded cap to protect his head. The wife of John Wesley was not unusual in boasting that when her babies were one year old *'they were taught to fear the rod and to cry softly'*. When a boy was five years old he was breached, that is taken out of skirts and put into breeches. This was a signal that the rule of women was finished. He was now considered old enough to help the family. His sister was expected to fetch and carry in the inn and help with tasks like the washing. She wore a cap on her head and a bibbed apron to keep her dress clean. If there was free time she might play with a wooden hoop or doll.

It is unlikely that Jeremiah and Ann could sleep late as they would be woken by noises from the street. Most people got up at dawn, awakened by sunlight or by the knocking of the watchman. There were the piercing cries of a milkmaid on her regular round with pails slung from a yoke across her shoulders. She chalked up on the door post the amount of milk for that week. Then there was the noise of carts rumbling past the window with men shouting at the horses, the barking of dogs and the cries of children.

Within the inn, cleaning could not wait until they woke up. English homes were said to be the cleanest in Europe after the Dutch. One foreigner wrote that *'Not a week passes by but well-kept houses are washed twice in seven days, and that from top to bottom; and even every morning most kitchens, staircase, and entrance are scrubbed. All furniture, and especially all kitchen utensils, are kept with the greatest cleanliness. Even the large hammers and the locks on the door are rubbed and shine brightly. English women and men are very clean; not a day passes by without their washing their hands, arms, faces, necks and throats in cold water, and that in winter as well as in summer.'*

Perhaps Ann slept later than Jeremiah. After a late breakfast of ale and cereal pottage, (a sort of porridge), we will imagine him spending much of the morning looking round the inn. To protect his shirt and breeches he wore an apron or smock rather than his coat and waistcoat and perhaps his turban rather than his wig.

The room next to the street downstairs was already open to the public. There was a large table in the centre with chairs arranged around it and a range to warm the guests. Servants took orders for drink or food and James Everitt bustled about to ensure that his guests were happy. One room was called the parlour and contained the better quality furniture. If the walls were not panelled they would be plastered with a mixture of lime and sand and hair. The plaster could be lime washed as was the outside of the house or had paintings directly on to it. It was unlikely that the windows downstairs had curtains. As the house had cellars the floor was wooden, but if there were no cellars then the floor would be beaten earth or lime ash which was hard enough to be polished.

The floor was swept with a broom but not washed as that made the surface muddy. Rushes were put on floors and fed to the pig when they were replaced. An alternative was sand. Sandmen called each week to sell it to the housewife. Better quality houses had floor tiles.

One of the first tasks was to inspect the written accounts of the Unicorn. They would probably be quite simple. Jeremiah might want to check on the amount of credit that had been given and hear what hope there was of receiving payment for the so-called *'desperate debts'*. He might agree with the decision to sell some of the goods that had been left in lieu or pawned. They would choose a hawker to buy the goods and sell them on. Then he would need to discuss the amount that was owed to maltsters and other suppliers.

He could also check that the taxes had been paid. The land tax was paid on property and on goods like malt. St Ives was lucky in that its taxpayers only paid half the national rate. For example when the government said that the tax must be paid at a rate of two shillings in the pound, St Ives paid at the rate of one shilling. This was negotiated by leading citizens of the town just after the terrible fire that engulfed the town in 1689. The rate of tax was never changed. However, St Ives demanded an extra two pence in the pound from those who owned property but did not live there. This was not in the act but was a local variant. It was not popular with taxpayers like Jeremiah but naturally reduced the demand on the residents. *'Yet I would have one thing mended which is to asses outlivers and indwelers all alike for it can be justly done and hurt none'*, had written Edmund Pettis. There had been a dispute in the previous year about the rates. Some inhabitants complained that they were rated to the full value of their holdings, others that they paid more than the value and that some paid less than half. Meetings were held at the Quarter Sessions to try and sort the problem out. In the end it was agreed that everyone would pay as if on an annual rent. Under the previous system a penny rate had produced a little more than seven pounds; the new rate raised more than fifteen pounds but it was so high that there were many evasions.

A rate also had to be paid to the overseers of the poor. This varied according to need. 1727 and 1728 were years that saw the death rate in the town nearly double and therefore the poor rate was higher than usual. *'A very sickly year al Europ over and abundenc dyd.'* A third tax

or rate was levied to maintain the parish church and churchyard whether people attended the church or not. It was very unpopular with nonconformists who had to support both the parish church and their own meeting house. Various people were refusing to pay it this year. Then there were additional taxes for the highways and the constables, both rates set by the Justices of the Peace.

Most people earned very little and only one in ten paid taxes. Innkeeping was one of the wealthier trades and innkeepers and maltsters paid a fifth of all the land tax assessed on St Ives. The size of the inns varied. The owner of the largest inn the Crown was charged £2.1s.6d, Jeremiah paid 10s for the Unicorn and the smallest the Three Tuns was charged 3s. To study the accounts and talk with his brother-in-law would take a good part of the morning.

When Ann was ready, she might look into the kitchen. Meat was roasted in front of an open fire on a spit that rested on hooks and was turned mechanically by a clockwork spit-jack. A cauldron of water was hung over the fire to provide hot water for washing or cooking. Smaller

25

pots of meat, or puddings wrapped in cloths were placed inside this cauldron to cook. Other pans were placed on supports or trivets that swung over the fire. Each day the cook made bread in the dough trough and baked it in the domed oven. She lit a wood fire inside it and when the temperature was hot enough, the ash was removed and the bread or pies put in. Once the food was in the oven the temperature could not be altered. There might also be a curing oven and one or two recesses for keeping salt and other materials dry. The house was well equipped with a brew-house, a coal-house and a turf house (to store peat). The beer was stored in the cellar in hogsheads and bottles. In London Ann had seen brick stoves built into a corner of the kitchen with fire baskets filled with charcoal covered by trivets on which pans were placed. This meant that the cook no longer had to bend down over an open fire. But good ventilation was required to remove the fumes unless there was a chimney over the stove.

The kitchen was the room in which the servants and family gathered. Older members of the family or friends might sit on benches at the well-scrubbed table to gossip or to eat. A dresser board displayed plates with cupboards and drawers underneath. There were candlesticks, kettles, basins and pewter plates as well as wooden trenchers (plates) on a rack . There was a copper warming pan to heat beds and a candle box for storing candles. A cat was curled up beside the fire. Its job was to catch the mice in the house and the dog dealt with the rats in the yard and stables.

They also wanted to look round the inn. In the room next the street they met old friends and customers. Jeremiah was particularly keen to see the state of the beer as it was crucial to the popularity of the inn. He counted the barrels as full, drawing or empty. Brewing was done commercially in a brew house but also in inns and private homes. The difference lay in the quantities. The Unicorn bought ground malt. A peck (two gallons) was added to a copper of water. When this boiled it was transferred to a mashing vat and four bushells of malt were added. (One bushell equals eight gallons.) Mashing meant stirring the liquid until it was like a pudding. More malt was added and then the tub was covered with a cloth for two or three hours. Hot water was next allowed to drip through the mash to be collected in the copper. A canvas bag of hops was added for flavour and the mixture boiled again. When the boiling was complete the liquid was transferred to another tub or vat and yeast was added for fermentation. After two to four days the yeast on the top was removed and the beer was ready to be put into barrels or bottles. These were then stored in the cellar. The minimum equipment required was a copper and its ironwork, mashing vat, cooler, working tub, trough and two pails.

They looked around the yard and stables and talked to the servants. Jeremiah's brother Joseph arrived to talk about farming. They saw the maids ironing. Their irons were either box ones which were heated by means of a piece of hot iron inserted at one end or smoothing irons, similar to flat irons heated on the range. The wash-maids had been in during that week. They came at dawn to do the washing perhaps once every five weeks and were paid six pence a day for their services. Before cotton became cheap, clothes were heavy to wash and done infrequently. It was a common practice for children to be sewn into theirs for the winter and men changed their shirt at most once a week.

Water was hauled up by bucket from the well and heated in great boilers. It was poured into troughs that were raised on low benches. There were two troughs in the barn for washing so that there was some protection from the weather. The clothes were first soaked to loosen the dirt and then beaten with flat bats. The washerwomen brought their small children to help tread the washing. The wealthier used soap but the cheaper alternative was a solution of ashes and other vegetable matter known as lye. It was made by putting ashes in a tub like a sieve to wash out the soluble potash salts. This liquid then ran into a second tub. Straw was steeped in the lye, then dried and slowly burnt and the ash from it produced a rich potash which softened the water. Fine linen after washing was soaked in starch. Then the clothes were rung out by hand and hung to dry possibly on hedges. Holly was useful as its prickles stopped the clothes falling off. Once the clothes were dry the maids of the inn ironed them in the kitchen.

Dinner was taken at midday. Judging by the number of tables and chairs in the bedrooms many visitors ate in their chambers. Because Jeremiah was staying in a working inn, I have assumed that he and Ann ate with the family and servants in the kitchen. This was *'a large roomy, clean kitchen, with a rousing wood fire on the hearth, and the ceiling well hung with smoked bacon and hams.'*

The English were well known for being *'great flesh-eaters'* who ate little bread and Jeremiah as a butcher enjoyed his meat. Today's simple meal consisted of a mess of pottage and meats *'plain roast and boiled.'* The food was placed down the centre of the table on great dishes. Everyone had their own plate and helped themselves from the communal dishes. They ate with knife and fingers and used a spoon for the pottage. The use of the fork was gradually spreading and Jeremiah might have used one in London. He could even have brought one as a present for his brother-in-law. English forks only had two prongs at this time. The French fashion of three prongs had not yet been introduced. Bread was handed round at the same time. They ate off pewter plates or wooden trenchers. In London Jeremiah knew of the fashion to serve ragouts in the French fashion but as a butcher he preferred the plain roasts of country cooking

After dinner Jeremiah was keen to take Ann round the town. He removed his apron, put on his coat and waistcoat and placed his wig neatly on his head. Then he sprinkled white powder or starch on it and did not worry if white dust covered the shoulders of his coat. He wanted to show his friends and neighbours that his move to London had brought him success although the generous proportions of his figure may have suggested this. She put pattens over her shoes to protect them from the muck on the street.

St Ives had been described as a *'little town but a very gay one. It has an extraordinary fine Market, especially for Cattle.'* Jeremiah was

pleased to hear that trade was improving. The market was popular and traffic on the river was increasing. Agricultural prices had been high for about ten years but had now dropped. Farmers were hoping that there would soon be an improvement. Labourers however benefited from the lower price of food. Inns were profitable. Indeed the Globe, the Crown and the Bell were being rebuilt. He knew that there were more people in the town. The diocese of Lincoln which included the parish of St Ives expected the vicar to estimate the population at regular intervals. At the last count in 1723 the vicar had said that the population had increased from 300 families in 1705 to 378, or perhaps 1700 persons. Of these perhaps 40 per cent (700) were below the age of 21 and 25 percent (400) below the age of 10, leaving an adult population of 600.

Let us imagine Jeremiah and Ann leaving the Unicorn to visit some people in the Bullock Market (now the Broadway) and to take supper with friends at the Salutation Inn. As they left the house they noticed the smells. Large numbers of cattle were traded on Mondays outside the Unicorn. It was good for trade but Mondays were noisy and smelly especially as there were few drains which were easily blocked and the surface of the market was not cobbled. In addition to the muck left by the market, household waste was often thrown into the centre of the street called the runnel that was only cleaned out properly when it rained. Human waste was collected by night soil men, although everyone knew that it was also secretly tipped into the street. The solid material was sold to market gardeners and the urine to tanners and other industrial enterprises. In 1814 the town appointed a scavenger without a salary "*to clean with his own labour the streets and lanes every week and day by day as necessary*" and to keep the compost and manure for himself. This might have been a new appointment or the first recorded entry of an existing position. Later he was instructed to clean the streets as early as possible in the week and that the cart was to immediately follow the besom (broom) to carry away the filth.

A newcomer was bound to notice the strong smells from the industrial areas of Tanners Row opposite the Unicorn. At the end near the Waits in an area called the Sands was a messuage (dwelling house with outbuildings and yard), now the site of the Norris Museum, occupied by Thomas Child and his wife Elizabeth. Thomas Child was a waterman and his property was on the river bank, a great convenience for his business.

Unusually for St Ives, part of this building was of stone, probably taken from an earlier medieval building. The upper storey was rebuilt in brick. Jeremiah and Ann called on the Childs who were relatives of his brother Robert.

Next door to the Child family was the house and yard of John Offley, a fellmonger, who cured skins so that the tanners could turn them into leather. Usually both these trades were sited on the edge of towns as they produced such unpleasant smells but easy access to water was also necessary and all these properties were on the river bank.

As soon as possible after the animals had been slaughtered the skins were collected for curing by salting or drying. The hides were soaked in a lime solution to loosen the hair and then hung on frames so that the remainder could be scraped off. After any remaining scraps of flesh were removed from the other side, the hides were scoured in a pit containing water and dung to remove the lime before being sent to the tanners. The hair was collected and sold for mixing with plaster for ceilings and walls. Horns were sold to make knife-handles and bones to make glue. The stench and flies from these processes hung on the air the whole time. There was a fellmonger like John Offley from Earith. When he died he had wool neatly stacked and sorted into different types, long skin, head, fleece and tail wool as well as 150 sheepskins. As a butcher Jeremiah was used to dealing with fellmongers and might discuss the trade with John.

Next door was a brew-house and malt house. Maltsters needed access to the river as the heavy malt was exported by water to London or the Low Countries. They noticed the strong smells and the belching smoke from the chimney. The brew-house belonged to Sir John Bernard of Brampton and was tenanted. It was a commercial undertaking selling beer to private individuals. The malt house was also a commercial enterprise supplying malt to inns like the Unicorn to make their own beer. The government encouraged malt making in East Anglia to absorb the excess grain. It was first dried, then germinated before being roasted in a kiln to prevent further germination. After it was ground up it was ready for brewing or for distilling. The waste was fed to pigs, sometimes said to be permanently drunk. A large part of government revenue came from excise duties levelled on the sale of alcohol. The heavy duty laid on brandy and imported wines led to the increased distillation of gin. Its production had become a successful sideline for brewers. It was a cheap drink frequently consumed in excess by the poor and causing major social problems in London. Maltsters would have been pleased that in 1726 the government had removed the excise duty on malt. However in St Ives land tax assessors had switched payment from small traders like bakers and laid it instead on maltsters. They argued that the maltsters could better afford to pay than the bakers. The opinion of the maltsters is not recorded.

    Jeremiah pointed out to Ann the home of the merchant Isaac Jones. Like other merchants he was a leader of the local community. His business benefited from access to the river from the back of his building and to the cattle market at the front. Next to him was the Mermaid, now belonging to the opticians. This was one of many inns owned by Mr Dingley Askham, another wealthy man. The new eighteenth century frontage had been added to the seventeenth century timber-framed building to make it look modern.

    Further along the street lived James Morton and his son who were both tanners and curriers. They tanned and coloured leather. They were Presbyterians like Jeremiah and he expected to see them on Sunday at the meeting house. They were wealthy tradesmen as the tanning of leather was an important industry in East Anglia. The hides were purchased from a fellmonger like John Offley. They had first to mill bark before soaking the hides in a series of pits filled with water and bark to prevent rotting and shrinking. The amount of bark or tannin was gradually increased depending on the intended use of the leather. Leather for the soles of shoes needed less tanning than good quality hide for saddles or belts. The process lasted several months. Eventually the hides were dried, dressed and dyed ready for sale. Tanners needed to have capital as the process of turning hides into leather took many months. Some of the finished leather was used in St Ives to make shoes, boots and saddles, although there was more selection in Huntingdon. Large numbers of hides were taken annually by boat from East Anglia to London. John

Beadles of Huntingdon is an example of a wealthy tanner who left skins valued at £350. His bark and bark-mill were valued at over £100.

William Warden, the dyer in Merryland, had a trade where some of the odours were less unpleasant. His premises ran down Dye Alley (Woolpack Lane) towards the river. He used dyes made from vegetables, lichens or insects. He made some of his own dyes. Like fellmongers, dyers relied on the night soil men to supply them with a steady source of urine to produce the green vegetable dye made from woad. In 1718 Warden's shop had been broken into and he lost several pieces of fabric, described as *'tammy yard width and lincy woolsy'*. Tammy was a glazed cloth made from wool and other fibres and linsey woolsey was a mixture of linen and wool. A reward of one guinea was offered for the apprehension of the thief. This was a large reward. When Samuel Papes was found guilty of stealing goods from Paul King his punishment was to be publicly whipped at St Ives on a Monday.

Jeremiah explained to Ann that the Unicorn was in Barkers Row, an old name recalling the bark needed in tanning and sold here long before his time. Most of the properties on their side of the Bullock Market were inns and provided the urine for their industrial neighbours opposite. To the west of the Unicorn was the Hoop at Blue Gate House, (now called Burleigh House), and the Axe and Compass, both owned by Edward Smith who was a maltster, yeoman and grazier. Mr Smith farmed at Warboys and was the coroner and bailiff for the hundred of Hurstingstone, one of the four divisions of Huntingdonshire. Like many property owners in St Ives his main home was elsewhere. His inn, the Axe and Compass, was in Old Yard, which was occupied by a further ten households, including the mother-in-law of Jeremiah's deceased sister where a visit was expected.

After this visit Jeremiah and Ann walked past the Unicorn, the Wool Pack and the Ram. (The stables and outhouses of the Ram are now Coach Mews.) Then they reached the Globe, a larger inn where the manorial court was sometimes held. An arch led from the street into a courtyard surrounded by buildings with a second smaller arch leading into the back yard with its stables and garden. The owners had recently rebuilt it. (It is now disguised by the present three-storied frontage of Wych House, the premises of the solicitors Leeds Day.) The town had recently cobbled the street from the Globe to the Crown which helped pedestrians.

Even so they walked with care as it was the responsibility of each householder to clean the section of the street in front of his door. This was an unsatisfactory system as not all performed their duties well. Sometimes pedestrians might meet "*unexpected chasms, or were offended or obstructed by mountains of filth.*"

Next was a substantial property, another inn - (the name is unknown) - rented by its owner to various people including Jeremiah's brother Robert and John Devonport, an excise officer. His was a Government appointment to assess the excise duty due from traders. For this, he was paid fifty pounds a year. As he had to buy his office there was an assumption that he was on the fiddle. Such places were generally gained by nepotism or favour.

As far as the Excise Office was concerned the country was divided into collections, then subdivided into districts and finally rides. Rides were often based in small towns like St Ives which was the base for two excise officers. It was the duty of the ride officer to survey every manufacturer of, or dealer in, an exciseable commodity and to record the charges due. He needed to have a good scientific knowledge as one of his tasks was to assess the amount of duty due on alcoholic drinks like beer. A contemporary writer had written that '*The English are taxed in the morning for the soap that washes their hands; at nine for the coffee, the tea and the sugar they use at breakfast; at noon for the starch that powders their hair; at dinner for the salt that savours their meat; in the evening for the porter that cheers their spirits; all day long for the light that enters their windows, and at night for the candles that light them to bed.*' He omitted bricks, coal, leather and glass. The excise officer was always unpopular and was moved frequently to avoid charges of corruption. Some were even murdered by smugglers trying to avoid the payment of duty.

After passing the lodgings of the excise officer they walked past the Three Pigeons and the Queens' Head (the Cow and Hare) with their boards hanging over their heads. Houses did not have numbers and strangers would recognise them by their signs. Where the central block of housing called Merryland intruded into the market area the road became narrower, and this was called Fanche Street. Here Jeremiah had to pass the White Bear, owned by an attorney in Huntingdon, and Vine Yard, which is now called the Royal Oak, until they came to the Crown Inn.

Print of the Salutation Inn

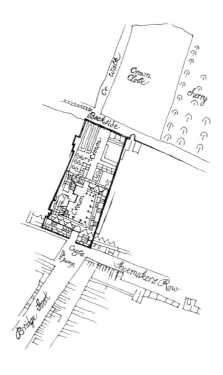

The Crown was the best inn in St Ives and the largest building. Its annual rental was £85, far surpassing any other building. The next highest (£38) was the inn near the Globe. St Ives Hall only had a rental of £26 and the Priory was rated at £20 the same as the Unicorn. The vicarage rated a lowly £10. The Crown had a prime position at the Cross facing down Bridge Street and also positioned on the road linking the Bullock market and the Sheep market. It was a three-storey building with a high arch leading into the courtyard. Two-storey buildings enclosed the yard with a covered arcade on two sides. Another smaller arch led to stables, granaries, a brewery, orchard and gardens. Across the road, known as backside, lay Crown close previously a bowling green. The complex included shops, taverns, warehouses and granaries. An inn like this would have cellars for beer and possibly wines although inns in St Ives rarely stocked wine or brandy. Of the surviving probate inventories for St Ives only two mention anything other than beer. In 1674 the inventory of Isaac Devies showed that he had French and Spanish wines, and William Lenton who died in 1723 had 7 quart bottles of brandy.

The Crown Inn had been occupied by William Bentley since 1718. He was a member of an important local family which was sometimes classed as gentry although in reality he was a successful urban tradesman rather than a member of the landed gentry. In the seventeenth century his ancestor Bartholomew Bentley had been a baker who served as churchwarden and vestryman. He had made an advantageous marriage to a wealthy woman and diversified into trading on the river. William took this one stage further by acquiring the Crown Inn and becoming a prominent local dignitary. In 1729 his son John had married and his father gave the Crown to him and his bride Dorothy. At present it was tenanted by Matthew Richards. On the same site was the barber's shop of Gilbert Cordel, and a cottage of Hanna Harrison.

Jeremiah and Ann passed the Crown to go next door to the Salutation Inn, the home of his friends. This was one of the oldest buildings in the town, also known as the Old House, the Old Court House or the Stone Hall and had been rebuilt in stone some two hundred years ago. It had an interesting history, as it had been the Court of Pie Powder. In the Middle Ages the fair at St Ives was famous for the sale of cloth and other goods. Merchants came from all over the country as well as from Belgium and France. The owner of the right to hold the fair had settled disputes in a specialised court called the Court of Pie Powder. The name was a corruption of the French 'pieds poudrées' or the dusty feet of travelling merchants. The court travelled with the fair. A case could be heard in St Ives and sentence passed in Winchester. It was now a building of two storeys with an attic. There was a cellar with rings on the walls, possibly once used as a prison. The actual hall for the court had long since been converted into cottages. One imagines Jeremiah and Ann walking upstairs to visit his friends in one of the two small oak-panelled rooms that may have once been the offices of the steward.

Thomas Swan was older than Jeremiah but the families had been friends for many years and were connected by marriage. He and his wife Sarah were friendly with the owner of the agricultural land that Jeremiah's father had rented. The couple expected Jeremiah to pay a visit and he brought a gift of tea and tobacco. Sarah and Thomas were both simply dressed. He wore breeches and a coat with plain waistcoat and an old fashioned full wig. Sarah had on a dark skirt and bodice with long sleeves that fitted over the top of the skirt and a clean white apron. Although younger women wore a hoop Sarah disliked it. She had crossed a handkerchief at her bosom and tucked it into a cross-laced corset. Thomas had a good reputation in the town *'as a man of fair character and credit among his neighbours'*. He had been appointed one of the two people to collect the tithes when the parish church was without a vicar and he had also served as churchwarden.

Although he had started life as a hatmaker he had left that trade to run the inn. Now hats were sold by someone from Huntingdon, who had a second shop in St Ives where he sold carolinas, grey felts, straw hats and chips in the fore-shop and manufactured hats in the workshop. He needed equipment like a press, planks, a kettle to steam the hats and a furnace as well as the materials. The three cornered or cocked hat had become fashionable in London and one imagines Jeremiah showing the hatter his new hat in the latest fashion. The high hat favoured by Puritans was now seen only in rural areas and mightily despised by anyone who fancied himself as being in the fashion. Labourers generally wore plain felt hats with large brims that they cocked up at the front so that they could see. These hats might have a buckle as decoration. Ordinary hats were made from felt as beaver was too expensive for all but the rich. Mercury was needed to cure the felt. This was a common cause of poisoning hence the expression 'as mad as a hatter'. Straw hats were originally worn by country people but had lately become fashionable. Ladies who wore the fashionable high wigs sported little flat straw hats like a dinner plate fixed to the wig, *'vastly becoming when they go out walking or make a visit.'* For most women a straw hat with a broad brim was more common with a cap underneath it.

Some years ago Thomas Swan had an adulterous affair with a married woman called Elizabeth Geary. This occasioned much gossip in the district. At the same time he and other officers of the parish had been forced to take Mr John Harkness to court for perjury. The surviving court documents give a vivid picture of the episode. Harkness was *'a man of very turbulent and unquiet spirit and of great wealth and riches. He was thought to have used unfair ways of getting money together.'* The vicar described Harkness as a man *'guilty of very foul and unchristian language so much so that few that know his temper will keep him company, he being very abusive and reviling in his liquor.'* Harkness planned to blackmail Swan because of his adultery hoping to persuade him to *'let fall the indictment'*. But the vicar persuaded the wronged husband to accept compensation of £20 *'so that he would not exsecute Swan for the crime of adultery'* and the vicar even loaned Swan £10 to help pay the husband. After Harkness was convicted of extortion at the Lent Assizes, he lost his temper and assaulted Swan in the public coffee house in St Ives. Once it became known that the husband had accepted money as compensation for the adultery of his wife Harkness had no means to blackmail Swan. The only way that he could get back at him was by himself accusing Swan of adultery in the ecclesiastical court.

To get his revenge Harkness initiated the case of adultery against Swan but he did not have any evidence. This, however, did not deter him. Before the case came to court, Harkness sent for Thomas Farthing a brickmaker who was under an obligation to him. Farthing had been recruited for the army possibly at the time of the 1715 rebellion of the Old Pretender. The government had demanded that a certain number of men were recruited from each parish. A ballot was held and if the man 'chosen' did not want to serve in the parish militia he had to find a substitute. Service in the army was regarded with great hostility because the army had a terrible reputation for indiscipline and lawlessness. The conditions of service were poor, the pay was low and the discipline harsh. Paupers, debtors, criminals and the unemployed were sometimes enrolled. Indeed a writer had described the army as *'a midden (rubbish dump) fit only for outcasts'*. Harkness as Farthing's employer, had helped to get him discharged and was now demanding his reward. He asked Farthing to go to the Bull Inn in Huntingdon the next day to meet a friend from Cambridge. He also offered him a crown (or five shillings) as though for a day's work.

At the Bull, the three men *'left the house and went through the yard into the back yard called the dove-house yard and walked up and down. Harkness lent against the yard bales'* and set out his plan. He wanted both men to swear that they had seen Thomas Swan and Elizabeth Geary together in a compromising position. Gilson began by saying that he had brought a letter to Elizabeth Geary. *'Knocking at the street door and nobody coming he opened the lower half door and went into a ground floor room on the left and called for Mrs Geary. With nobody answering he went out again with a desire to go home to his lodging but perceiving the light of a candle through a keyhole of a brewhouse or back room he went to the door and opening it he saw against a copper Thomas Swan and Elizabeth Geary very close together he with his breeches hanging about his heels, she with her coats up to her breasts so that he saw her thighs bare. Whereupon he slipped back again into the entry and pulled the door close behind him and in a very little time opened it and looked in and called her name and he saw Swan pulling up his breeches.'* This was not enough for Harkness who said *"Can't you as well say then that you see him knock her and there's an end?"* To which Gilson replied *"Let them judge that when I'm examined in court".* Then Harkness replied again *"Can't you say you see him knock her and there's an end?"* And then Gilson made answer *"Yes, Sir, I can."* Harkness then demanded that Farthing corroborate this version. However he had misjudged Farthing who was an honest man and when asked to swear to this story in court he told them exactly what had happened.

The adultery, blackmail and threat of proceedings in the church court must have caused a lot of pain to Sarah Swan. Divorce was rare and only possible for the very rich who could afford a private Act of Parliament. Nor was the husband's adultery grounds for divorce. As Dr Johnson wrote *'The chastity of women is of importance, as all property depends on it.... Wise married women don't trouble themselves about infidelity in their husbands ...The man imposes no bastards upon his wife.'* Public opinion believed that a woman was at fault if her husband committed adultery. The only ground on which a married woman might win some sympathy was that of brutality. Henry Geary who had been cuckolded by his wife might have suffered public punishment. It was the custom for the neighbours to perform 'rough music', that is to raise a din and parade obscene figures, to shame the cuckolded husband into putting his house in order. As a husband he was entitled to confine his wife at home against her will and even beat her as long as he used a stick no thicker than his thumb. (This is the origin of the phrase 'rule of thumb'.) If he had accused her of adultery and sued her lover for damages she could not give evidence nor call witnesses on her own behalf.

Elizabeth and Henry Geary lost their child and Henry died after a few years. Their great enemy, John Harkness, had died ten years ago. Much later, perhaps as a means of showing his gratitude to the church, Thomas Swan gave the church a great branch (candlestick) and two

sconses (wall lights) at the desk, pulpit and clerk's desk. One imagines the rest of the congregation sitting in semi-darkness while candles burnt down in their sockets.

As country people still kept to the old custom of eating their dinner at two or three pm, his hosts might offer Jeremiah and Ann a supper of cold meat and pies with bread and cheese. Pies were not served in slices as they are today, but the lid was opened and diners helped themselves to the contents with a spoon. In their youth, bread would have been made from a mixture of grains called maslin but nowadays people preferred the soft white bread made from wheat. The meal was accompanied by beer. Perhaps they discussed the tragedy in their lives in that they had no surviving children to inherit the inn. As Thomas felt old and unwell this was a matter of great concern to him. He had decided that the inn should go to his brother and in the event of his death to his nephew.

After a pleasant evening we will leave Jeremiah and Ann to say good night. Candles cost a lot of money and few people could afford to stay up late. Nor would they wish to traverse the streets in the dark for fear of stepping in some dung or falling down a hole. When they returned to the inn, they might take some bread and cheese up to bed with them in case they became hungry in the night. They would put them inside a cupboard with the candle and the lidded beer tankard on top.

Bridge Street

After a good night's sleep Jeremiah and Ann were up early to see the servants at their work. Because it was the fair on Monday there was more work to do than usual. The town would be very busy and the Unicorn expected to be full of visitors. Saturday was the day for serious cleaning. Floors were swept, fires relaid, and chamber pots emptied into the cellar or cesspit in the yard. The cook had started the bread at dawn and set the meat on the spit. Others went to make the day's purchases. If meat had not been finished the previous day it was put into a salting tub to preserve it. Keeping meat or fish fresh was an important task. After a morning's work the family dined together at 12 o'clock. Today they enjoyed a hearty dinner of boiled salt beef cooked in a pot inside the cauldron of boiling water. A few vegetables tied in a cloth had been added to the pot together with the pudding. The English were famous for their puddings. Today's version was a fairly heavy recipe. Flour, milk, eggs, butter, sugar, suet, marrow and raisins were tied in a pudding cloth and plunged into the cauldron. Everything simmered gently together.

After dinner Jeremiah set out to pay a formal visit to Mr Richard Huske, the steward of the Duke of Manchester. For this visit Jeremiah ensured that he was dressed in his best clothes with his wig neatly powdered. Ann we will leave at the inn to help with the preparations for Monday. When Jeremiah reached the top of Bridge Street he saw the wooden Cross that may have been set up at the time of the grant of a market charter in the Middle Ages. (The modern reminder of it is the black cross that is painted on the frontage of Woolworths.) Every town has a place where people, especially the young, like to gather and it was at the Cross in St Ives. As a child Jeremiah had heard the strange tale of a young man who had crucified a cat here more than an hundred years ago. It had created quite a stir at the time and news of it was sent to the Lord Bishop of Lincoln. The church was always suspicious of anyone making fun of the crucifixion. There was also a complaint about crowds of *'divers idle and disorderly persons'* who *'assemble every day and evening and particularly on Sundays about the Cross.'* The Vestry meeting wished them to be dispersed by the constable or prosecuted. One of the town pumps was at the Cross and Jeremiah saw people carrying home buckets of water.

Just by the Cross was the Red Cow kept by Joseph Hardmeat, a Quaker. He also owned the six tenements attached to this inn on the south side of Fanche (Crown) Street where two barbers, a tailor, a shoemaker and a widow lived. Everyone recognised a barber's shop by its pole. He was not always busy as people only expected to have their hair cut when the moon was full. Jeremiah walked past the premises of Joseph King, another Quaker and ironmonger. His open-fronted workshop displayed the hand-made items for sale, chisels, axes, wedges, files, locks, keys, awls, flat irons, scissors, knives and nails. The area behind was hot and noisy with the furnace blazing and workmen shaping metal on anvils. Some pious tradesmen rose early and closed their shop for an hour between nine and ten for prayers attended by the family and servants. Joseph King preferred to get up even earlier and hold prayers before trading started.

Next to him were some drapers, one of the wealthier trades in the town. The first, (now Tindall's the stationers), belonged to William Hatly from St Neots, who bought the property in 1708. In 1719 he had been elected churchwarden, the most prestigious post in the town only held by the wealthiest people. He and William Barnes were responsible for the construction of the gallery in the parish church. His neighbours, the Reads, were also drapers. They owned the present Oxfam shop and Bryants the department store. Jeremiah could see one of their tenants Henry Patrick sitting cross-legged on his table at the window. All garments were sewn by hand. A man's suit was expected to last fifty years and was the most expensive purchase after a house. Clothes were refurbished, left in wills, cut down to fit a smaller person and sometimes sold to a dealer. Even as wealthy a man as Samuel Pepys bought clothes second-hand. Perhaps Jeremiah touched his hat to Patrick, as he passed his shop and entered the next building.

Mr Richard Huske was under-sheriff in 1732 to Mr Roger Thompson another townsman of St Ives, who was the sheriff of Huntingdonshire, the Isle of Ely and Cambridgeshire. The sheriffs were responsible for the organisation of elections, including their site, timing, conduct and supervision. As eighteenth century politics were frequently corrupt, sheriffs had great opportunities to abuse the system to the advantage of themselves and their political masters. Richard Huske had married the daughter of John Prudent, a wealthy butcher in St Ives, and thus acquired the messuage in Bridge Street with its shared access to a well in the back yard leading to Woolpack Lane. They would have no need to use the common pump. Prudent had fallen out with his son, Joseph, who only inherited five shillings "*being all I intend him out of my personall estate by reason of extravagency and undutifulness towards me and his mother*". The old man left his property to his daughter and on her marriage it passed to her husband. As Mr Huske sometimes acted as steward for the Duke of Manchester, he was possibly the most powerful man in the town. Rather than conducting his official business in the Toll Booth opposite, we will assume that he was receiving visitors at home.

The Duke of Manchester, who lived at Kimbolton Castle, owned the manor of St Ives as well as many other manors in the vicinity. He was such an important man that anyone writing to him used the most obsequious language. One worried steward once wrote to him when there had been trouble over the levying of a rate. He finished his letter in these words '*All whichwith my selfe and service I here submitt to your good Lordshippe with protestation that I have and ever shall honour and love you and I hope you will not beleeve any ill information against mee ... before you heare mee ....*' Through his steward the duke levied tolls on those who wanted to sell in the market. He received the tolls of waggons crossing the bridge and from barges tying up at the wharf. He owned the manorial court and was entitled to all the profits from it. Most property in St Ives was copyhold. There were two charges to be paid on copyhold property: a small fixed annual rent and a fine paid on entry to the property. The fines were negotiated with the steward. They had doubled and sometimes trebled over the years to the great advantage of the duke. For example Jeremiah might know that the annual rent for the property once belonging to a certain William Whittle was eleven shillings and sixpence. The entry fine had increased from £12 to £46 and such a sum had to be paid whenever there was a change of ownership or tenancy. These were substantial sums. Someone had calculated that the duke's receipts from St Ives were roughly £400 per annum. These tenancies had to be registered in his court and were legally held by copy of court roll. The records were written in Latin, which was unintelligible to most people. Under the Protectorate of Oliver Cromwell, who had farmed in St Ives for five years in his youth, it was ordered that writing should be in English so that ordinary people could understand documents. But as soon as Charles II was restored to the throne the clerks reverted to Latin. Many people looked forward to the day when it would change back to English for good.

Of course everyone knew that the duke did not keep all this money for himself but used some of it to pay for improvements in the town. The pound for straying animals had been rebuilt in the time of his father, and a clock, dial and alarum installed at the Cross soon afterwards. There had been a different kind of timepiece or bell that only rang at the hours of 4 and 8. Now townspeople knew the time throughout the day. Clocks were set by a sundial. This meant that time varied across the country according to the position of the sun. The greatest use of the alarum was in the event of fire, as in 1689. The duke had recently paid for the bridge to be rebuilt after the damage caused in the Civil War and for the wharf to be rebuilt and widened. There was also a new weathercock on the tollbooth in Bridge Street that showed the four points of the wind, a novelty to the townsmen. So although the duke received a lot of money from the town he did pay for some improvements.

Jeremiah did not expect to see the duke himself but he felt the need to pay a formal visit on Mr Huske. As befitted his rank the steward was dressed in a full-bottomed wig with long curls falling down one shoulder and over his back. His coat was long sleeved with huge cuffs folded back and decorated with gold trim and buttons. His full coat reached below his knees and was left open to reveal his satin embroidered waistcoat. Tied round his neck was a white neck-cloth with lace edging. His matching breeches finished above his black silk stockings. The whole effect was designed to reinforce the difference of rank and wealth between him and the ordinary townspeople.

There were others waiting to see him. There was bad feeling in the town over the activities of the bailiffs of the market. James Burford and Samuel White had signed a lease on the market and fairs with the duke for £105 per annum. It is possible that Samuel White largely put up the money while Burford did the work. The latter rented a tenement at the Red Cow with Jeremiah's brother and was a barber surgeon by trade while Samuel was a wealthy draper. As bailiff of the market Burford was trying to increase the receipts. He wanted to charge for the right to display goods for sale on the pavement in front of a shop. The shopkeepers were objecting as they maintained the pavement themselves and had never paid this charge before. Edmund Pettis, a surveyor and cooper, was keen to tell Jeremiah about it. *"I told 'em. It had not been demanded of me above forty years. Nor had they a right to any there nor none I wo'd pay. Then they said they wowd distrain and did in my Lord's name and carried it off. I told them it was a mean act and that the hand that carried it away would bring't again."* He wanted Mr Huske to intervene with the duke on his behalf and was demanding that Burford return to him in person the scythe handle that he had taken. Pettis later succeeded in his demand. He invited Jeremiah to visit him next week to see his maps of the town.

Another cause of bad feeling was the ten extra shops that had been built and let in the market. They cut off the existing houses from the open area so that their trade had suffered. Burford wanted to set up two more shops. Again Pettis was eloquent on the subject. *"The neighbourhood had taken umbridge"* he told Jeremiah, *"and had told the bailiffs that they were a public nuisance for they hindered the sight and communication of that part of the street. They were threatening to proceed with an indictment at the Assizes on the grounds that the Lord's grant from the Crown was for the Monday market and the two fairs at Whitsun and St Lawrence.*" The townsmen were in belligerent mood and were demanding that all the shops should be removed. They wanted the lord to be informed and expected him to take action. They were demanding a promissory note of £10 to be forfeited if the work was not done to their satisfaction.

The registration of property was less contentious. Any transfers of copyhold property had to be registered with the steward at the next manorial court. This took place in October and was called the View of Frankpledge, a medieval term for an annual meeting of the manor for every male over the age of twelve. At the meeting last October there had been twenty six jurors enrolled to listen to cases involving transfers of property, thirteen in St Ives and thirteen in the agricultural part of the parish, called Slepe. These jurors were substantial householders like Jeremiah's brother Robert. Last October Richard Huske had registered his own acquisition of the Chequer Inn. The annual rent was eight shillings but because of his position he was not charged an entry fine. Property could be transferred in between courts provided it was registered at the next one. Joseph King, the ironmonger at the corner of Bridge Street, had only bought his property on the twentieth of April. He would need to attend the next court to register it.

An important resident in Bridge Street was Robert Robinson, a haberdasher, who sold small articles of dress. His goods were cheap, varied and popular. His opening hours were from eight in the morning till late in the evening. Shop assistants lived with his family. They were well turned out, with their hair curled and powdered by a barber. Periodically Robinson went to London to purchase more stock. Because he could read and write he was often employed to value the property of a deceased person for probate. A tax of ten shillings was due on goods valued at more than £20.

Then there was Ephraim White. He had been a wealthy draper who also owned the Bull Inn on the opposite side of the street, forty-two acres of arable land, some meadow, Dunkirk House and farmyard and two tenements near the wharf. He had died in 1731. One son Ephraim had left the town for Southampton, while another Samuel lived in a large house near the parish church, rented the market, owned a brew-house in Kings Lynn and more property in Hemingford Grey. The eldest son Benjamin was a draper. In his counting house he entered the rents from his properties and the names of those buying on credit or borrowing money from him. His customers lived in Huntingdonshire, Cambridgeshire, and in the fens as far as Kings Lynn. In effect he was a banker, moneylender and draper.

Benjamin had taken charge of the newly built wool-house. This was a large building which contained store-rooms for hundreds of pounds of wool. There was a chamber where the wool was sorted into different types according to the fineness of fibre and length. After sorting, it was washed to remove the grease and dirt. Wool from sheep reared in the damp climate of England contained a lot of grease to protect the animal from rain. The best agent to clean the fleece was stale human urine that had been kept in a closed container for a fortnight to allow ammonia to develop. After soaking in this, the fleece would be repeatedly washed to remove the dirt. It would then be hung out to dry. In another room the wool was combed to straighten the fibres before spinning. John Belton was one of six woolcombers in the town. His work was slow and time-consuming. The wool was placed between two carders which were wooden tools covered on one side with hooks. The carders were pulled across one another to straighten the fibres. This was done six times before all the wool lay in one direction. It was then removed and rolled into hanks for the spinners. He carded in his *'working shop'* where he also sold small knitted items like caps and hose (stockings) for adults and children. He was wealthy enough to have a house with six rooms, a kitchen, a parlour with a bed as well as chairs, pictures, window curtains and even a looking glass, a chamber with a bed and three rooms used for work. He employed apprentices to help with the more mundane tasks. He put tops out for spinners and owned a horse for making deliveries in villages. He also rented a furnished cottage to a tenant. The hempdresser James Constable was less wealthy. His first room doubled as a kitchen and living room. There were two other rooms used for sleeping, a very small buttery, a workshop and a barn.

The carded wool was taken to the spinners' cottages. They were paid when the hanks were collected. Some spinners and weavers owned

their own wheels or looms, but the poorer ones rented them. George Chaplyn lived in a cottage with three rooms, a bedroom with three beds of different sorts, another chamber with one bed, some other items of furniture, hemp, coal and wool, and the 'lowe' room which had chairs, eight pieces of pewter, two chamber pots, a spinning wheel, a cupboard and a pail. The family cooked, ate and worked in this one room. They used the other two rooms for storage and for sleeping. The value of all his goods was £7 and poor as he was he was owed £6. The spun yarn was taken to a weaver. Jeremiah might remember the time when his father went to appraise the goods of a weaver called Nathan Neave. He had made his will when '*told by his master Henry Nickolls that he was not likely to live long in this world.*' At least he did not live long enough to suffer from the painful disease called 'weaver's bottom'. Neave had left three pounds and fourteen shillings. Forty shillings were spent on his burial and to pay his few debts and his master inherited the rest which included his most precious possession, his Bible. He lived in two rooms, the 'low room' being used for living and cooking which had a hearth, a lodging room with a straw bed and his shop with its looms. His cottage would be crowded and busy. '*The wheel going at the door, the wool and yarn hanging up at the window, the looms, the winders, the combers, the carders, the dyers, the dressers, all busy and the very children, as well as women constantly employed.*'

From the point of view of these masters the financial risk of their business was considerably reduced by this system. If the demand for thread or cloth was low, they had no craftsmen to pay and the cost of keeping an expensive loom idle was the risk of the individual weaver. For spinners and weavers life was far more precarious. Their low wages were subsidised by the poor rate which helped them out when there was no work.

Much of the wool was sent to John Day, a wealthy factor or middleman in Norwich. He in turn supplied White with different types of fabric. He stocked sixteen different types of cloth, including nankeen, (a yellow cloth used for breeches), ribbed druggits, (a coarse woollen cloth used for floor or table coverings), burying crepe and curtains. Most of these fabrics were fairly coarse and suitable for everyday wear. Silk, satin, velvet and lace were unobtainable in shops in St Ives.

Times had changed to such an extent that almost everything of an ordinary man's clothing was manufactured in different parts of the country. His coat was made of woollen cloth from Yorkshire, the lining from Berkshire, the waistcoat of callamancoe from Norwich and breeches of drugget from Devizes. In addition his stockings probably came from Westmoreland, his felt hat from Leicester, leather gloves from Somersetshire, shoes from Northampton, buttons from Macclesfield or metal ones from Birmingham, garters from Manchester and linen for his shirt from Lancashire or Scotland. In the same way a wealthy tradesman's wife might have a gown of mantua-silk made in Spittlefields in London with an under-petticoat of black callamancoe from Norwich, quilted at home with Manchester cotton. An under-petticoat might be made from flannel or swanskin from Salisbury or Wales. Ordinary stockings came from Tewkesbury or the better woven ones from Leicester. If she had wrapper or morning-gown it might be of Irish linen printed in London.

As a Presbyterian Ephraim White had been well known to Jeremiah. We will imagine that he crossed the road to Thomas White's coffee house in the Mitre (now the Trustee Savings Bank) next to the Bull Inn. Coffee houses had become popular in London at the end of the seventeenth century and had then spread to smaller urban centres like St Ives. They offered an alternative venue to inns. Men used them like a club and gathered there in the afternoon while the ladies took tea at home. In London Whigs and Tories patronised different coffee houses, as did traders like booksellers, stockjobbers, doctors and merchants. Newspapers and journals were circulated through them; they were used as postal centres, business addresses, and gambling dens. A French visitor saw them as *"the seats of English liberty where you have the right to read all the papers for and against the government"*. They might serve the exciting new drinks of Turkish coffee, West Indian cocoa or Chinese tea. Chocolate had at first been marketed as a medicine rather than a social drink. It was said to be a powerful aphrodisiac. Coffee on the other hand was seen by some as a powerful stimulant for rheumatism. Others thought it was the enemy of the nerves. Only the rich could afford these drinks which were alternatives to beer.

One can imagine Jeremiah entering a large room, with an open fire, a deal table and chairs. Men sat and smoked Virginian tobacco in long clay pipes, took a hot drink and discussed the day's news. Jeremiah wanted to know the local news and to meet innkeepers and farmers. For his own part he brought news from London. The English were very interested in politics and Jeremiah had brought with him a copy of a London newspaper. Coffee house gossip said that the present king was *'a humourless, choleric, conceited bore and womaniser. A man of routine and a penny-pincher, he was banned from court as Prince of Wales after he had quarrelled with his father.'* Meals were at specific hours and he hated to be kept waiting. Each Saturday he thundered off to Richmond with his cavalcade of precisely dressed officers. He and his father King George I were known as Dunce the First and Dunce the Second. Jeremiah also brought news that the famous man Sir Isaac Newton who discovered the laws of gravity had recently died.

In a corner Jeremiah saw Mr Thomas Dawkes, an apothecary and surgeon. Doctors frequently used coffee shops for consultations. Most learnt their trade in an apprenticeship. Although they had a certain status in the community they had been apprenticed to a surgeon or apothecary in the same way as Jeremiah was apprenticed to a butcher. It is possible that Dawkes was the apprentice of John Litchfield a surgeon who had died in 1729 and whose goods Dawkes had valued when he died. Dawkes had five mortars to mix his drugs as well as scales, weights and surgical instruments. He specialised in purges, vomits and bloodletting which was thought to remove pain and fever. He also treated many illnesses by bleeding with leeches. As an apothecary he had some knowledge of chemistry. He made and sold painkillers, opiate powders, pills and cordials. New cures were Jesuit's bark (quinine) for fever and compounds of mercury for syphilis. People believed that blood should be let in the spring so Dawkes would still be busy. He also undertook basic operations but as the notion of cleanliness was not understood all surgery was very risky. Samuel Pepys was one who successfully survived the removal of a large gall stone. Dawkes's fee was ten shillings a visit, beyond the means of most townspeople. A problem for doctors and most tradesmen was the collection of fees. When John Litchfield died he left book debts of over £61 and other debts called 'desperate' to the value of £77. His widow did not have high hopes that she would ever recover these debts. Dawkes had resolved that he would not give credit so freely. What he earned from medicine was supplemented by his draper's shop. It was fitted with a counter, boxes and drawers for the sale of cloth, handkerchiefs, gloves and stockings.

Those who could not afford a doctor for a birth used a midwife licensed by the Church of England. There were two in St Ives, Susan Dickinson and Mary Pope. Both were widows supporting themselves as best they could. Mary Pope lived in rented accommodation in Free Church passage and Susan Dickinson near Cank Alley. They each sold beer when they were not helping in childbirth. Although Widow Dickinson owned her own cottage her tax bill of two shillings the half year was reduced by six pence.

An alternative possibility for the sick was to visit a barber surgeon, like James Burford, the bailiff. He specialised in bloodletting, extraction, cleaning and scraping of teeth, nail paring, ear waxing, shaving of beards and heads and wig-making. Others might be tempted to buy patent medicines like *"pulvis vulnerarius or infallible styptick powder which instantly stops the most violent flux of blood etc. It could be had at Mr White's Coffee Shop in St Ives, at Mr Stocker's Bookseller in Godmanchester and at his shops in St Ives, St Neots and Huntingdon."* Then there were others who used folk remedies, healing by herbs, charms or witchcraft. The Honourable John Byng wrote that *'I drank snails' tea for breakfast for my chest was sore.'*

After smoking a pipe, drinking some coffee and spending a pleasant hour with friends, Jeremiah continued down Bridge Street. We will assume that he looked across to the west side of Bridge Street. He could see the perukemaker Samuel Emerson. He worked downstairs in one room and the family lived upstairs in two rooms. This meant that all food had to be stored upstairs but cooked downstairs. Water was taken up

in pails and slops carried down, taken through the shop and dumped outside. On the front of his shop hung his painted sign of black and white perukes. Wigs came in many styles and were worn by most people, even labourers and there was a lively trade in second hand wigs. Emerson had several apprentices. One was shaving a customer's head and beard. Samuel was fitting a wig for a customer. Another apprentice was painting a wig with a liquid pomade to keep the curls in place, then covering the customer's face while he dusted the wig with grey or white powder. In the back of the workshop Samuel's wife and daughter were weaving the net frame on which the curls were mounted. The net panels were sewn together to form the shape of an individual head. An apprentice was twisting the wisps of hair on to long silk or cotton threads to be sewn on to the net frame. The hair was curled by frizzing irons or put into split curling papers. The flat top of the wig would be ironed by a warm flat iron. On the bench a young boy was carding the hair and sorting it into wisps of different sizes. He tended the stove used to dry the hair and the copper to boil it. Emerson also sold the cheaper worsted wigs of Edward Willshire, a jacey weaver. He was a much poorer man whose loom was in his kitchen and twisting mill for thread in a garret.

Three other wealthy families had properties in Bridge Street. Dingley Askham Esq had married the daughter of Mr Robert Clark, one time steward to the Duke of Manchester. They had lived at Somersham before moving to the manor house at Conington. Her marriage portion consisted of 370 acres of land, the second largest holding in St Ives, as well as eleven houses or farmhouses, the Wool Pack, Ram, Mermaid and Chequer inns and the big house in Bridge Street. His property in St Ives was valued at £2,200, a huge sum of money for the time.

The Askham's neighbour was William Barnes who owned the corner house, now called the Manor House. This was a timber framed house two storeys high with attics and tiled roof. It was built in the shape of half an H with wings extending to the west. Jeremiah had always admired the grotesque figures carved on the projecting gables. He knew that some of the rooms were richly decorated with carved ceiling beams, stone fireplaces and panelled walls.

William Barnes was a wealthy maltster. His father had been a baker who also owned barges on the river and dealt in other goods. His son followed in his footsteps. He owned the properties on each side of Bridge Street, called Wharf Corner and Bridge Foot. He could watch his three boats loading his malt for transport to London. He was involved in many aspects of town life. He had been churchwarden, a juror at the Assizes and a vestryman as well as a juror for the manorial court. He had other houses and stalls in the market, the Mansion House near the river where he lived as well as a business making starch. He held mortgages for townsmen and had given credit to many people in the surrounding villages. These could be small debts like 7s 2d owed by Thomas Brown a brickmaker or £7 8s 10d lent to a boatwright Henry Nicholas or £328 16s borrowed by Mr Hatly.

St Ives was a busy inland port. Goods arriving by sea at Kings Lynn were brought up the Ouse on lighters. Coal was one of the important loads. It was used in many industries, like malting, tanning, ironwork and brickmaking. The more traditional peat fuels from the fens, known as turf, firing and sesses, were still popular but coal was more efficient for industrial purposes. The flow of the river had been a major concern to traders for centuries. Millers wanted to keep back a pool of water to drive their waterwheels, but watermen needed sufficient depth to transport their heavy loads. Prior to 1723 the river at St Ives had become so shallow that boats or lighters could only pass up the river when there was a flood or at high tide. This had badly affected trade in the town. In 1723 the staunch (lock) was rebuilt and the water penned. It reopened to everyone's relief on June 15 of that year. Those who were most concerned to improve the flow were the coal merchants of Bedford. The conflicting needs for water, between the millers, the watermen and farmers meant that they had to negotiate with one another to reconcile their different needs.

View of the manor house from the Quay

    Because roads were so poor, heavy goods were usually taken by water. Farmers who lived near a river could easily transport their grain. Those further away needed waggons, an expensive purchase only possible for big farmers. Farmers in places like Brington or Bythorn preferred to convert their arable land to pasture and concentrate on raising cattle and sheep which could walk to market.

    As Jeremiah reached the end of Bridge Street he came upon a bustling, noisy scene. He could see boats tied up at the quay with men staggering under the weight of sacks of coal, baskets of pots or fish, or bags of hops, malt or corn. He might even see loads of timber from Norway or grain from Poland. There was much shouting and swearing. Some huddled together to negotiate prices and deliveries. Porters hung around hoping to get work. Carts and waggons were unloading goods.

He could see men hurrying to one of the local inns for a drink or staggering out the worse for wear. They could choose from the Ship, the Chequer, the Bricklayers Arms or the Maidenhead on the Quay. He recognised Richard Stocker manoeuvring away from the quay on his front lighter, with a second one trailing behind, while his apprentice, William Banton, encouraged the horse that was towing them. The horse first pulled the boats through the water to the other side of the river and then clambered out to walk along the tow path on the Hemingford side. The boats commonly carried 14 to 16 tons and the watermen expected to receive 3d per ton for each passage. Although Richard Stocker owned his own boats the goods he carried belonged to wealthy gentlemen like Mr Denne of Tempsford or Mr Wilkes of Bedford.

At least the river was navigable at the moment as floods were a constant problem. Jeremiah was pleased to see the bustle and the trade. He perhaps greeted Thomas Childs who was connected to him by marriage. He was walking back from the Ship, his home in Water Lane, having left his grandson Joseph guarding the boat. Watermen were away from home so much that a brief few hours with the family were a pleasure to be savoured. Thomas Childs was unusual in St Ives. He was wealthy enough to qualify to serve on the vestry at the parish church yet he could not write his own name. He always signed with his mark and someone else wrote '*Tho Childs sen His mark*'. However as reading and writing were seen as separate skills to be learned at different times the chances are that he could read. He was able to do his accounts in his head and memorise all his transactions.

His son Thomas was involved in a case of defamation at the moment. Anne Bentley who lived with her husband Griffin in the first house on the quay had called Elizabeth Child *"a common strumpet"*. This was a terrible insult because it harmed her good name. To clear herself she had taken her case to the church court which would decide on the rights and wrongs. A paper had been fixed on the house door to inform Anne and Griffin of the pending case. Watermen's wives seemed free with their tongues. There was another case pending between the wife of the waterman Reuben Eldred and Richard Lewis, the starchman who worked for Thomas Barnes.

Jeremiah saw the Baptist chapel at the end of the Quay. In the seventeenth century both the Baptist and Quaker sects had been particularly active in Huntingdonshire. Henry Denne, one of the national leaders of the Baptists, was also the leader of the local church which worshipped at Fenstanton and Caxton. After the Toleration Act of 1689 his son John became the leader of the church which met in his granary in St Ives, now the masonic lodge on the waterside.

Baptists searched the Bible for guidance. They held that baptism could only be administered according to the example of John the Baptist and Jesus. Believers were publicly baptised in the river Ouse. Whilst Baptists demanded strict obedience to their rules they were generous in their charitable work. For example, John Offley and his wife had been excommunicated in the seventeenth century for interpreting the words of the Bible in a different way or in the words of the Baptist register *'denying all the ordinances of the Lord'*. But they showed their generosity in the case of Mary Whittock. She was a travelling pedlar whose case was brought before the Fenstanton General Baptists. They recorded that *'she is destitute of harbour, and her mother being very sick, and her children small, and the ways dirty, she is not able to travel from place to place as she hath been accustomed'*. John Denne agreed to provide her with accommodation and the church voted to give her twenty shillings to enable her to start up in trade again.

Unlike the worshippers at the parish church who lived in the parish, nonconformists like Baptists also came from the surrounding villages. By the time of Jeremiah's visit only five families in St Ives regularly attended the chapel. This is reflected in their choice of trustees. One of the four trustees was Jonathan Denne, the son of the founder of the

sect. His wealth came from the river and from agriculture. He employed watermen like Richard Stocker to take his loads between Kings Lynn and Bedford. Another trustee, Mr John Cropper of St Ives, was wealthy enough to be the owner of a *'good second-hand chariot'*. Mr Robert Knightley was a butcher who worked in the Butchers' Shambles. The last trustee was Christopher Ashton of Fenstanton who also owned land in St Ives. They had connections with Baptists at Sutton. When William Jenoway died in 1725 he left sufficient land to produce an income of six pounds a year which was to be paid to the Anabaptist minister at St Ives to preach at Sutton *'as long as the World shall endure'*.

Beyond the Baptist Chapel, Jeremiah could see the narrow lane known as Fish Street, (Wellington Street) and beyond that Water Lane. Many watermen and their families lived here. Their homes were small cottages cramped together and sometimes flooded when the river was high. The only large building was Dunkirk House and farm owned by Ephraim White.

At this point we will imagine Jeremiah starting to walk back to the Unicorn. On his way up Bridge Street he avoided the two houses of the Harkness family, the great enemy of his friend Thomas Swan. He passed the Bull Inn (West End Stores), belonging to his old friend,

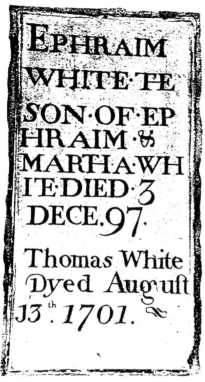

Tombstone of Ephraim White's children

Ephraim White. This was one of the big inns in the town and was severely damaged in the terrible fire in 1689. It had been rebuilt with sash windows which are still visible on the first floor. Its staircase had turned balusters, with moulded rails. Doors were panelled and the fireplace had fashionable Dutch tiles. Ephraim had given part of the back garden of the Bull Inn to his fellow Presbyterians so that they could build a meeting-house in the lane behind, now called Free Church Passage. He had designed a side entrance for his family from their garden. A stone tablet now in the Free Church commemorated his two children buried there.

Near him lived a Quaker, John Abbott, whose family had lived in St Ives for more than a century. He was interested in new technology and was variously called a tin-man, a tinplate-worker or a brick-maker. One imagines that his yard produced a lot of noise, heat and acrid smells as pots and pans were 'tinned' or coated with a fine layer of tin to prevent corrosion from acid foods. His workmen suffered physically working in such difficult conditions often described as hellish. There was no health and safety legislation. The making of tinplate (thin, high quality iron sheets) was a craft that had not long been started in Wales. Abbott bought the sheets and made them up into different items. He had an apprentice, Robert Stacy, to whom he had promised his tools, tin sheets and tin wire to the value of £5 on his death so that he could continue in the trade.

Abbott also owned the chandle house at the back of Butchers' Row behind his house where he made tallow by rendering down fat. The tallow was turned into soap or mixed with wax for candles or rushlights. They made candles by dipping a wick into melted fat and then leaving it to cool and solidify. The process was repeated until the candle was thick enough. These were kept in a candle-box which was a common possession. Rushlights were a cheaper version of the candle. The pith of rushes was dried and dipped in mutton fat. It was laid in a piece of hollow bark to dry. It burnt in an iron-holder for half an hour. His other business was brickmaking. Houses in St Ives were generally built of timber with lath and plaster between. But since the Great Fire of London and the fire of St Ives in 1689 less combustible brick was preferred. Bricks were made in kilns on what is now the golf course. There was another brickmaker called Thomas Stadderd who was seriously ill. He had two brick kilns heated by turf. The lease of the kilns was £13 per annum, a substantial amount of money. He made bricks and roofing tiles (pantiles) and owned his own small fleet of boats so that he could deliver bricks and tiles to his customers. He lived near to the brick kilns in a large house by the parish church. Bricklayers tended to earn less than brickmakers and lived in little houses in the back streets.

John Abbot's father Daniel had been persecuted in the seventeenth century because he had refused to attend the parish church or to pay church rates. He had been arrested in 1670 at an illegal meeting by a constable and fined five shillings. When he refused to pay some of his goods were taken for sale at the Crowne Inn in Huntingdon. Abbott's family maintained that not all the goods were sold and that a man called Edward Hansome secretly took home a new lanthorne under his cloak. Quakers frequently suffered sharp practice at the sale of their goods. Under government pressure persecution was increased in the 1680s. Daniel was again fined for not paying a church rate. He was prosecuted by Edward Young, Aaron Browne and Obediah Gee who were the churchwardens that year. Obediah Gee was a founder member of the Presbyterian church in St Ives. Forty years later there was probably wariness between the Abbott family and the Presbyterians. Daniel Abbott had died in 1721 leaving only £35 which included the cash in his purse, his clothes, the goods in his (work) shop, the contents of his house and the brew-house. His son John, although much wealthier, followed his father in his beliefs and was a trustee of the Quaker meeting house.

His neighbour was Robert Lancaster, a leather cutter. A whole hide was too expensive for self-employed shoemakers to purchase, and so leather cutters bought prepared hides, cut them into smaller pieces and sold them to shoemakers. As Lancaster lived in a prestigious part of the town his trade must have been good. His large yard and stables stretched back into the Sheep Market near the Shambles where he had a two storey cottage. This gave him access to Bridge Street and the market. Next to him was the Tollbooth where tolls were paid for trading in the market and on the river. The building was also used as the town lockup. Jeremiah had heard that after the fire it was decided that the walls of the Tollbooth facing the Cross were to be left unchanged. On top of this two storey building townspeople could see the small bell-tower with steeple and the new weathercock. This part of the town had only been rebuilt in 1705 some sixteen years later.

The Tollbooth was next to the Le Legg Inn rented by a Quaker grocer called Peter Clay who was refusing to pay the church rate. He had both an inn and a shop. The grocer's sign of a sugar loaf hung outside. As a young man he obtained his stock by going to London once or twice a year. He bought the goods and paid half their price with the rest due when he returned for more the following year. Now that he was older he preferred to do business by letter especially as he knew a trustworthy merchant in London. His goods were loaded on to a ketch on the Thames, offloaded at Kings Lynn and brought up river to St Ives. The fair and weekly market were vital to his trade. These were the times when he sold most. He sold some things during the week at his shop, called '*a continuous market*'. Before the Whitsun fair his apprentices had worked long hours to prepare and package goods like sugar, tobacco, brandy, nails and prunes. His most profitable line was tobacco. He could buy it at wholesale prices as St Ives was a river port with two excise officers. Quakers had a reputation for honesty. He set his price '*at one word without bargaining or abatement*'.

Most grocery shops sold dry goods rather than perishable items which were usually bought in the market. A grocer in Huntingdon sold a mixture of items that included dry goods, like salt, soap, candles, sugars, pepper, spices, strong water (spirits), vinegar, anchovies, capers and also fresher items like hops, cheeses, honey, plums, apples, nuts and eggs. His drawers contained thread, laces, worsteds, pins and needles. There were items for cleaning like brushes, mops and lamp black. He also sold earthernware, the dye indigo, tobacco and pipes, pitch and tar, and even powder and shot. Thomas Figgis a grocer in Hemingford Abbots, had a smaller range of goods for sale, including almonds, ginger, silk, sugar, fish-line, nails and vitriol or sulphuric acid sometimes used in medicine. These were typical items for sale in a general shop.

At this end of Bridge Street there were several properties belonging to members of the Society of Friends or Quakers. They were a close-knit group of about ten families who had all suffered from persecution. They felt safer living near one another in the town. The name Quaker comes from the shaking that characterised their behaviour at early meetings. They rejected the established church in the belief that they must model their lives on the authority of the scriptures. The word and will of God were central to their lives. God's divine intervention could be detected in every aspect of human behaviour. God's anger could be calmed by prayer and fasting. They had no formal services, no sacraments like baptism and marriage and no ministers.

Some Quakers were poor labourers but the movement also attracted wealthier people. They were respected by the townsmen for their honesty, goodness and charity. Originally they sold goods at fixed prices but some copied their neighbours and allowed customers to haggle. They stood out because of their plain old-fashioned clothes and their high hats. Their manners were aggressively humble and their speech plain and old fashioned, so that they used *'thee'* instead of *'you'*. They insisted on calling the town Ives because they did not recognise saints. In earlier years they had been abusive to priests and in trouble with magistrates when they refused to swear an oath or serve in the military. These things irritated their fellow townsmen but they also respected them as decent, peaceable people. Jeremiah knew that they were a small exclusive group who did not seek to make converts. If they married 'out', that is married someone who was not a Quaker, they were expelled from the meeting.

In 1690 they had built their own meeting house with its graveyard on freehold land behind the market in Chapel Lane at a cost of £140.15s. It was rebuilt or extended in 1725 for £90.17s. This small building in a rich reddish brown brick was not in the style of the parish church, but had a large open hall with gallery above. Today it is called Gateway House. The lovely eighteenth century bricks have been covered with ugly concrete and the building is in poor condition.

Although Quakers were no longer persecuted for holding illegal meetings some still refused to pay tithes. They held regular meetings at which items of business, doctrine or behaviour were discussed. They made decisions about the purchase of land for Quaker burials and the construction of meeting-houses. They considered applications for marriage and registered births and burials. The grocer, Peter Clay, represented the Ives meeting at the quarterly meeting at Huntingdon. At one meeting Thomas Cox who was apprenticed to a woolcomber in Earith *'desired to go to America.'* Many Quakers had emigrated to Pennsylvania where they were free to worship without restriction or fear of persecution. Another asked permission to go to Pennsylvania but in fact went to live with a woman who was not a Quaker and was forced to leave the meeting. Communal worship and regular meetings were designed to enforce a strict adherence to their beliefs. As practising democrats they sometimes had problems with people who spoke too much at meetings. Frances Field was criticised for wilfully *'opening her mouth too largely at many times even beyond the guidance, conduct and authority of God's holy and pure spirit.'* Two friends were asked to see her *'hoping that through the striving mercy and love of God she may reclaim herself and refrain for the future such extravagencies of an erring, seducing and by-leading spirit.'* Quakers lent one another money in times of need and apprenticed poor children so that they learnt a trade. In such ways they gave one another support even if they lived somewhat differently from their neighbours.

By now it was twilight and Jeremiah was keen to return to the Unicorn. The inn would be busy with merchants and visitors arriving for the fair on the Monday. He turned left into the lane called Merryland to make a last call at the Three Tuns, another inn owned by Mr Isaac Fisher (now called Nelson's Head). Mr Fisher had borrowed £80 on the security of his inn from Edmund Pettis. It was a good investment for the old man. The present tenant was John Wills whose wife Mary had a daughter in April. She was extremely glad that her labour was over as childbirth was a dangerous time for a woman. There were few painkillers and she knew that her friend, Jeremiah's sister, had not only died in childbirth but also lost her child. A mother-to-be would sew a slice of witch-elm into her petticoat, to bring good luck in labour. The only anaesthetic available was alcohol. Now she and the family rejoiced that a healthy baby was born. She had been helped by relatives and a midwife but none had any ideas about hygiene and did not even wash their hands. Had she been the wife of a wealthy man she would have remained for some time in the birth-chamber surrounded by the perfume of spices like coriander, violet and rosemary. Here she would have entertained visitors and offered them sugar coated confits. But as the wife of a working innkeeper she did not have that luxury. She was expected to be up and about as soon as possible. This Saturday was twenty eight days after the birth and she had been to church for the ceremony of churching which was both a service of thanksgiving and the occasion when the new mother was welcomed back into the community. She had attended the church with the women present at the birth, especially the midwife. Now it was a time for feasting and merriment. Jeremiah had been invited to celebrate the happy event. He shared a quick drink before returning to the Unicorn.

Whit Sunday

Everybody woke early this morning as Whit Sunday was a special day in the religious year. The morning service in the parish church commenced at nine but the hour of the evening service varied according to the time of year. In May the evening service was at six. It was a more popular service because the prayers were shorter. In the winter it might be held at three in the afternoon to save on the cost of candles. Parishioners were expected to attend both services. However it is hard to imagine the entire population of 1700 in the church. Officially those who did not go to church could be fined but in practice the very poor and those called undesirable were not pressed to attend. Most trading, work and entertainment were banned on Sunday. A Swede who lived in England wrote that *'Nothing could be more wearisome, more silent, more gloomy than an English Sunday'*. Undoubtedly some visited alehouses on the one day of the week when people did not work. On this occasion even if there were nothing to do in preparation for the fair there was a feeling of anticipation in the town.

Dissenters or nonconformists were allowed to attend a licensed meeting house as an alternative to the parish church. However they were barred from holding public office by the Test and Corporation Acts unless they were prepared to take communion at the parish church once a year. A certificate of baptism from the parish priest was also required. As nonconformists were often wealthy tradesmen this could be a disadvantage. Mr Thomas Houghton a wealthy Presbyterian solved the problem by having his daughters baptised in the meeting house and his son at the parish church so that his future career could not be adversely affected. As I have assumed Jeremiah to be an ambitious man, I have made him attend the parish church. He might wish to mix socially with his betters who were there. There was a saying that *'The Dissenter's second horse carried him to Church'*. Jeremiah's brother-in-law was not in the same position and we will send him to the Presbyterian meeting house as usual.

Ironically, once freedom of worship had been granted by the state, the number of nonconformists began to decrease. Periodically the Bishop of Lincoln asked vicars for the numbers of worshippers. Whereas sixty Presbyterian families had been recorded in 1705, by 1723 there were 42 or roughly 190 people; the number of Quakers had halved to 45 persons and there were only 20 Anabaptists. One cause for the decline in numbers may have been that people preferred the relaxed atmosphere of the parish church where attendance was expected at services but little was demanded in the way of strict behaviour. People expected to attend for baptisms, marriages and burials, and for the churching of women after childbirth. They did not want the constant interference of the minister, long sermons and detailed explanations of biblical texts. Some complained that meeting houses were not catering for *'the plain people of low education and vulgar taste.'*

The attitude of Samuel Pepys towards the church was typical of many. He observed the outward ceremonies but without any great conviction. Sometimes he went to church for an assignation with a woman he fancied. He usually went twice on a Sunday but was mainly concerned that he sat in a pew that reflected well on his social standing in relation to the others present. He criticised sermons, *"an ordinary lazy sermon of Mr Mills"* and often found it difficult to stay awake. *"A young simple fellow did preach (and) I slept soundly all the sermon."*

The ringing of the bells summoned the people to church. The tenor bell had cracked some years ago and the churchwardens had contracted with Henry Penn, a well-known bellfounder at Peterborough, to melt down the six old bells and make eight new ones. When the bells were rehung there was a dispute over the cost. The churchwardens complained that they were not as ordered and only offered £63. Penn

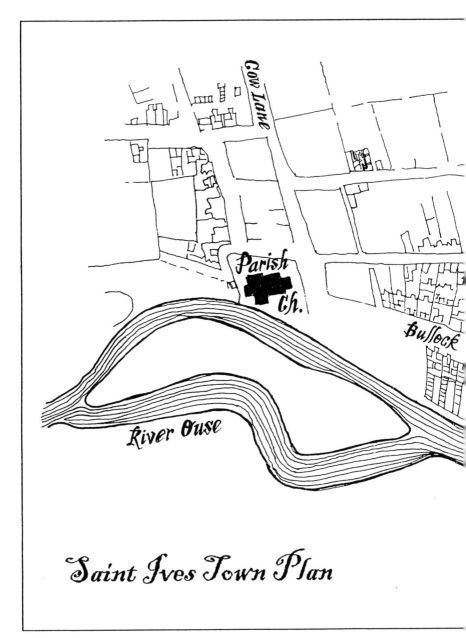

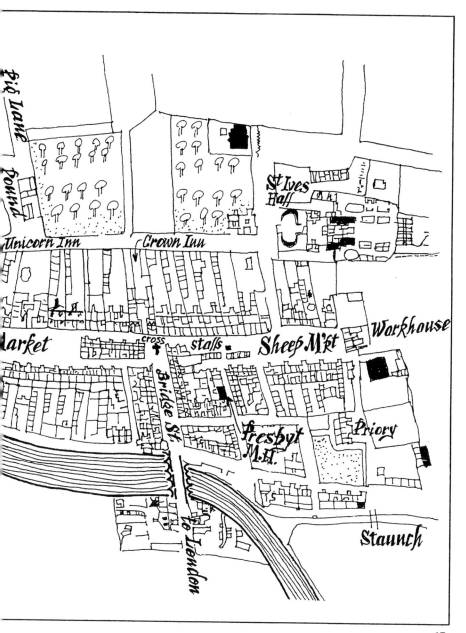

wanted £70. He took the churchwardens to court in London. The members of the vestry meeting agreed to stand surety with the two churchwardens to pay their costs. The case was referred to the Assizes at Huntingdon and ultimately Penn won his case. The town first demanded a rate of one shilling in the pound to cover costs and then raised it to one shilling and threepence. *"The founder was sick to death at Huntington at the time of Triall when twas over He was told he had got the cause Penn answard twas to late he was to far gone that his Hart was broke Therefore could do him no good twas decreed that the widow Penn and the Town should bear each their own Charges. Only the Town to pay her the damage given on the trial. This cause cost a prety sume of money But the poor widow got but very little or none of it. As for Penns death twas no loss he was a vile man & gave trouble where ever he was consarnd but was never so well yoak't before."*

Summoned by the new bells Jeremiah and Ann left the Unicorn to go to church. As they walked west the houses became smaller. They passed the Town Waits and the Middle Waits made up of seven tenements let to various people. These small cottages were the homes of bricklayers, a cordwainer and a blacksmith. They saw the cockpit which would be busy tomorrow. Nearer to the Church was the larger house of the brickmaker Edward Stadderd. After the Waits they enjoyed the newly laid gravelled walk to the church. When the vestry paid for the road from the Waits to the Church to be gravelled the overseers wrongly charged the cost to the vestry. This had to be corrected as the inhabitants were expected to repair their own piece of road.

They saw a wedding party coming cheerfully down the path. John Steel and Elizabeth Burket had just recited their vows in front of the vicar. Family and guests having scattered grains of wheat for fertility were now walking to her father's home in the Sheep Market for the feast. After the wedding cake was cut she would pass pieces through her new ring and give it to her unmarried friends so that they might soon be married. Her family had provided as much food as they could afford. When all had finished eating there would be dancing, singing and practical jokes. Finally they would escort the young couple to their new home singing obscene songs.

The church of All Saints was in the main a fifteenth century building with some more recent additions. At the time of the Reformation the rood screen, statues and stone altar had been destroyed. Later a Puritan minister had bought a communion table which was put in the body of the church. It had since been replaced by a new altar at the east end of the chancel. Within the last ten years a gallery had been constructed inside the church, the east gate built, and a new copper fane put on top of the steeple. The steeple was not in a very good state and a few voices grumbled that they would soon have to pay to repair it.

As it was Whitsun, there were many attending the morning service. Communion was only administered four times a year in St Ives, the minimum requirement. The vicar could refuse communion to parishioners if he felt they lived *'open and notorious evil lives'* or *'betwixt whom he perceiveth malice and hatred to reign, not suffering them to be partakers at the lord's table until he knew them to be reconciled.'* He always hoped that a public rebuke would prompt people to change their behaviour.

Once inside Jeremiah had to decide where to sit. The gentry like Sir Edward Lawrence or Mr Robert Piggott probably had special high box pews. Unlike the rest of the congregation in winter they could warm themselves at a stove in their curtained privacy. They might arrive late and leave early. Lesser folk were relegated to pews or long benches. As All Saints had begun to replace the benches with pews we will assume that Jonathan and Ann were shown to a place in one of them. The poorest people and young persons, segregated by sex, were probably in the new gallery. Here they might sit as a captive and unwilling audience under the beady eye of their employers. It was the duty of the churchwardens to keep order amongst the young. I imagine that this unattractive role was delegated to the Sexton as the churchwardens were men of some dignity in the town.

Attendance at church was seen by the educated as a means of controlling ordinary people. *'It is certain the Country-people would soon degenerate into a land of Savages and Barbarians were there not such frequent returns of a stated time, in which the whole village meet together in Church with their best faces, and in their cleanest habits, to converse with one another upon indifferent subjects, hear their duties explained to them, and join together in Adoration of the Supreme Being.'* Or as a popular rhyme says

*'And though I've no money, and tho' I've no lands
I've head on my shoulders and pair of good hands.
So I'll work the whole day, and on Sundays I'll seek
At Church how to bear all the wants of the week.'*

The vicar entered dressed in a long black gown and white surplice with starched preaching bands falling from his neck. On his head was a curled and powdered wig parted in the middle. We can imagine him processing in behind the choir, with the clerk in front. The vicar took the service with responses led by the parish clerk. When he preached he climbed into the oak pulpit carved in 1620 with the clerk at a desk beneath him. Behind him was the 'branch' given by Thomas Swan, newly polished for Whitsun.

Most parsons did not write their own sermons but read published homilies. In 1718 Mr Bariff, a grocer in St Ives, had advertised the sale of *"private manuscript sermons in a legible hand and never in print."* At Whitsun the vicar preached on a common theme, that property and authority were divinely ordained. It was part of God's world that ordinary people should accept their position in life and defer to those above them. One bishop had claimed that '*God has distributed men into these different ranks, and has formally put the poor under the superintendency & patronage of the rich.*' This is illustrated by a prayer from a popular religious book the New Whole Duty of Man. "*Oh God, I believe that for just & wise reasons thou hast allotted to mankind very different states and circumstances of life, & that all the temporal evils which have at any time happened unto me, are designed by thee for my benefit: therefore, though thou has thought fit to place me in a mean condition, to deprive me of many conveniences of life, & to exercise me in a state of poverty, yet thou has hitherto preserved & supported me by thy good providence, & blessed me with advantages above many others... "* It was the birthday of the late George II so the vicar reinforced this message by praising the deceased king and encouraging patriotism. Psalms were sung in a metrical version accompanied by a choir or fiddlers but there were no hymns. The Church of England rejected them on the grounds that they were of human rather than divine composition. Some parish churches had a table in the middle of the nave for the communicants but not at St Ives. After a bitter struggle in the previous century over the placing of the table, the altar and sanctuary were now railed and communicants came forward to kneel and receive the sacrament.

On this Sunday the vicar had a special announcement to make. By the terms of Dr Robert Wilde's will, dated 10 August 1678, fifty pounds had been left to the parish church to purchase a piece of land with an annual income of £3, payable at Easter each year. The vicar and churchwardens were to use this money to purchase *"six plain and well bound Bibles in English never exceeding the price of seven shillings for each."* They were to choose twelve persons, six males and six females, as are of good report, born in the parish, more than twelve years old and able to read the Bible. On Whit Sunday the vicar announced that on Tuesday they should *"resort at nine of the clock in the morning to the Church and then and there take their lot at the Communion Table for six Bibles and no two to cast twice for that year."* According to the terms of the will the vicar had to supervise the Bible dicing and deliver the sermon .

On this Sunday I have assumed that the Squire Sir Edward Lawrence and Mr Robert Piggott, the vicar's patron, were present. The sermon on obedience to God and one's superiors would have been very acceptable to them. At the end of the service they expected ordinary people to hang back to allow their families to leave. Men doffed their hats and bowed or knuckled their foreheads while their wives and daughters curtseyed. Such important men were not often in town and even the vicar was careful to treat them with respect because of the power they exercised. Jeremiah was recognised by the parish gentry, like Mr Thomas Houghton and Mr Thomas Barnes, who were tradesmen like himself. These were the people who on death were buried inside the church and commemorated by plaques on the walls. The names of those who had made donations to the church in the past were listed with the details of their gifts on the north wall.

As they walked out of the Church by the west door Jeremiah pointed out to Ann the handsome house recently built by Mr Samuel White, the brewer, (now called Barnes House). On the corner of the nearby lane, called Poor Lane, was the small home of the Selbys who sold home made confectionery at a stall in the market. As it was Sunday the sweet smells of sugar and flavourings did not linger on the air. Poor Lane was home to many families crowded together into eleven tenements. One was the Parkinson cottage. His grandfather had been a brazier, (a worker in brass), who had for a short time been a figure of ridicule. There had been name calling in the street between two women. Mary Enderby, the wife of a clockmaker Robert, had called another married woman, Elizabeth Edings, a *"hussif"*, or *"brasen face"*. She said that Elizabeth *"had been common enough. You have lain with Ned Parkinson."* The witnesses testified in the church court that Mary had accused Elizabeth of adultery. She had said that Elizabeth *'had lain with Ned often enough and that he was seen to come out of her bedfram and upon the bedside putting his breeches on.'* Elizabeth said that it was a lie and was supported by her husband. She was *'of good report and reputation amongst the better sort of her friends and neighbours'*. Such an accusation was taken very seriously as a woman's reputation was highly prized and to be defended in the church court if necessary. There was another case pending between Margaret Whiteside and Hannah Bolton. When Hannah, the wife of a wealthy woolcomber, was called a whore by Margaret Whiteside she and her husband decided to take the case to the church court. It would be heard after Margaret's baby was born.

Just north of Parkinson's cottage was the vicar's house, rebuilt in 1708. Vicarages were often not much more than thatched cottages with farm buildings attached. As the vicarage in St Ives had been rebuilt in 1708 it may have been reconstructed in brick in the new style. It had outhouses, a dovehouse and an orchard of one and half acres. Where a vicarage was well endowed with land, the vicar either farmed the land himself or let it to others. Unfortunately for the vicar of St Ives the amount of land attached to his vicarage was minimal. He received a small amount from two ecclesiastical taxes and more from bequests. The

Barnes House

major part of his income came from tithes. There were two types of tithes, the greater and the lesser. The greater tithes in St Ives had been surrendered to the Crown at the dissolution of the monasteries. They were separated from the church and sold as a separate entity. They were owned by Mr Piggott of the Priory and Squire Lawrence and were equivalent in value to 250 acres. The vicar received the smaller tithes estimated at 99 acres of land. Tithes were paid in kind or in money in lieu.

    In the taxation records for St Ives Edmund Pettis valued the vicarage at £100 but was forced to reduce it to £20. He wrote that *"I lay'd the Vickerig at a 100£ per anum Thay at but 20£ so hear's no contradicton but faver."* The vicar was delighted. When he subsequently complained that he had not received the money due to him from bequests Pettis was quick to explain that the money had been invested in land in Bedfordshire which paid him £12 per annum. As he was also vicar of the nearby parish of Yelling, he was not a poor man. John Wesley's father in Lincolnshire had £200 per annum on which he was able to support his wife and those of their 19 children alive at the time.

Most parsons saw themselves as belonging to the 'county elite' and socially superior to local tradesmen and farmers. They were generally university educated and were given the status of 'honorary' gentlemen as were lawyers. It was a suitable job for someone of gentle birth who may have been more interested in the income from his glebe land and in the pleasures of social life than with teaching Christian tenets to ill-educated parishioners. Many took an active interest in politics, hunted, farmed and dined with the Squire.

The vicar of St Ives the Reverend James Dodgson was satirised in a book published in the mid-eighteenth century under the name of Mr Swallow *"whose Dexterity and Assiduity at Backgammon, Dancing, Drinking and Wrestling had few Equals"*. He was born in Lancashire and educated at Cambridge where he became known for his public wrestling. He and others used to go into the country and strip for wrestling. *"Everything that could give the least Alarm to Modesty was bundled up in a Handkerchief, by those that were naked, and in their Shirt-lappets by those that were otherwise, on purpose to puzzle the impertinent Guesses of ... prying Hussies."* There were suggestions that he was also interested in other women as a verse told how his wife Judith, described as a *"turbulent spouse"*

> "*One day in her Tantrums had got*
> *And vow'd that her husband had been with a Blowse.*"

After obtaining a degree Dodgson had to support himself for five years until he could be ordained. Many would-be priests supported themselves by acting as servants to gentlemen commoners at the university for the requisite five years. Before ordination he had to secure the title to a curacy.

> '*When Dukes or noble Lords a Chaplain hire*
> *They first of his Capacities enquire.*
> *If stoutly qualified to drink and smoke*
> *If not too nice to bear an impious Joke*
> *If tame enough to be the common Jest,*
> *This is a Chaplain to his Lordship's Taste.*'

Dodgson was lucky when he became chaplain to the Honourable Lady Stanhope. On his tombstone this chaplaincy is recorded before his vicarages of St Ives and Yelling. This is similar to the epitaph of a Mrs Bates which stated that '*by means of her alliance with the illustrious family of Stanhope, she had the merit to obtain for her husband and children twelve several appointments in church and state.*'

A chaplain lived in the great house but was treated as little better than a superior servant on a salary of £10 per annum. In one case a chaplain was sent "*from the Table, picking his Teeth, and sighing with his Hat under his Arm, whilst the Knight and my Lady eat up the Tarts and Chickens.*" Dodgson was again fortunate. Somehow he met Robert Piggott owner of the Priory who presented him to the living at St Ives in 1717. In 1722 he also obtained the living at Yelling about an hour's ride from St Ives. This suggests that he knew the right people.

It was not uncommon for a vicar to hold two or three livings at the same time. It increased his income and he could always employ a curate to perform some of his duties. He only expected to pay the curate £10. On this pittance he might live in rented accommodation with scarcely sufficient to support a wife and family. Many curates increased their incomes by teaching or trading. A curate called Mr Hemingway had died in 1678. Besides the clothes he was wearing and his money, he left a few meagre possessions; two shirts, four handkerchiefs, four caps, two hats, one pair of boots, one pair of stockings and one pair of shoes. The lack of furniture suggests that he lived in lodgings. But he also left an extensive collection of books, the mark of an educated man. He owned more than eighty books ranging in subject from Homer's Odyssey and the Roman poet Juvenal to Bibles, twelve prayer books and many different works of theology. The books were much more valuable than his personal possessions. No-one in St Ives had the necessary expertise to put a value on his library and his executors called on the services of Henry Dickinson, one of the leading booksellers in Cambridge and Thomas Lynford, a fellow of Christ's College, to make the valuation.

The vicar had many responsibilities. He had religious duties to perform, a social position to maintain and he was the head of a unit of administration of the state. His religious duties were not too demanding and may have left time for the drinking and dancing of the accusation. He was required to perform marriages, baptisms and burials, to preach on Sundays, and to visit the sick but only if requested. He was also expected to see that the catechism was taught to children. This took place on Wednesdays and Fridays in Lent. Although catechisms were printed, the priest would read the sentences aloud and the class learnt them by heart. For this form of teaching it did not matter whether people could read or write. Many of these duties were delegated to a curate especially as Dodgson had two churches.

In Tudor times the government expected parishes to provide for the poor, to maintain the highways and to keep order, under the supervision of the Justices of the Peace. All who lived in a parish were subject to the authority of at least four officials – churchwarden, constable, surveyor of highways and overseer of the poor. The vestry coordinated these activities. At the annual meeting on April 13 1732 sixteen men had signed the vestry book. The vicar's name came first. On the occasions when Sir Edward Lawrence, the Squire, or Mr Dingly Askham, a major landowner, were present they signed their names before the vicar as their status was higher. The rest were wealthy inhabitants who were not elected but derived their membership from the tenure of particular properties. One of them was Jeremiah's brother Robert.

The vestry meeting dealt with a whole range of events relating to the life of the town. They were in effect the town council, although the

Plaque inside All Saints Church

privately owned manorial court was responsible for the market, bridge, wharf and agriculture. The vestry meeting supervised the overseers of the poor and chose the parish constables. When it was decided to purchase a fire engine it was the vestry that raised eighty pounds to cover the cost. They organised a school for five poor boys and annual civic events. It was their responsibility to pay when vermin like polecats, weasels and hedgehogs were caught and destroyed.

These might be called the miscellaneous duties of the vestry meeting. More specific tasks related to the church. Two churchwardens were appointed annually. For some years the merchant Isaac Jones had been appointed by the vicar and the draper James Fisher by the parishioners. They had conducted the case against the bellfounder William Penn with its attendant worry and expense. As churchwardens they had responsibility for the fabric of the church and the conduct of its religious life. They were expected to provide wine and bread for communion, to allocate seats in the church and administer the churchyard. They were responsible for the administration of the rites of baptism, marriage and burial. They had to ensure that burials were completed between sunrise and sunset. They had various reports to make about the state of the church and the parsonage or the number of dissenters in the parish. They were assisted by a Sexton called John Constable and a clerk Charles Eaton who probably did most of the work.

The Sexton and his wife received one shilling a quarter for 'scouring the communion plate every month'. Her husband received eighteen shillings for his duties as Sexton. His new coat was provided by the vestry. The material for his coat cost £1.3s.6d and John Wright received 4 shillings to make it. Fees paid to the Sexton in 1807 give a fuller idea of his job. His annual salary was increased by fees paid for services. For example, he was paid 1 shilling to ring the 'passing bell' for the death of a man or woman and 2 shillings for ringing the bell and digging the grave. For washing a surplice four times a year he received 10 shillings and cleaning the branch of candles given by Thomas Swan twice a year 5 shillings. The bellringers were paid 10 shillings in May and October. Another report says that the *'ringing days were only to be the King's Birthday, the 5th of November and the 29th of May.'*

Charles Eaton was the parish clerk in 1738. The vestry decided that he should be paid £5 to educate six poor boys chosen by the churchwardens and principal inhabitants of the parish. At first he had

Parish Chest for storage of documents and valuables

only received £1.5s.0d for one quarter as some of the parishioners were against the payment in spite of the vote of the vestry. Afterwards he received his money regularly. The number of boys educated in this way was minuscule in comparison to the number growing up in the town. *'St Ives though exceeding populous, and of pretty extensive traffick, is altogether destitute of everything in the shape of a free or charity school.'* Not everyone agreed about the importance of education. Some thought that if a poor boy was educated *'the less fitted he'll be to go through the fatigue and hardship with cheerfulness and content.'* There were private schoolmasters like the Quaker Christopher Kay who had lent money to Jeremiah's father but at least a quarter of the principal inhabitants could not write their own name.

The churchwardens needed money to perform their duties. £25. 8s 8d per annum came from the 'Town Estate', but it was shared between the vicar, the purchase of Bibles, the bell ringers and the alleviation of poverty. Churchwardens were allowed to levy a rate to cover expenses related to the church. All but the poorest had to pay. It was bitterly opposed by dissenters, especially Quakers. Seventeen people had recently been taken to the church court in Huntingdon for refusing to pay. Many of them were substantial men in the community.

Meanwhile Jeremiah's brother-in-law and family were attending the Presbyterian meeting house in Prudent Alley, (now Free Church Passage), leading from the Sheep Market to the quay. The Presbyterians had a long history in St Ives, dating back to 1612. Their meeting house was a simple eighteenth century building with a small yard to the south. It had been built in 1691 on land given by the draper Ephraim White. Two doors opened on to the lane and double doors led from the meeting-house to his garden. When he gave the piece of land for the meeting house, the first trustees were himself, his son Samuel White a hosier, John Payne a baker, James Morton the currier in the Bullock Market and James Nutter a sievemaker. Like the Quakers and Baptists they were a close-knit group.

At services in the meeting-house men and women sat separately, the mens' pews having hooks for hats. Some meeting-houses had great square family pews, lined with green baize and studded with brass nails. The communion table was in the middle with seats around it for singers, led either by a precentor at a desk or by a solo instrument like a bassoon.

The pulpit stood against one wall. Above it was a heavy wooden canopy or sounding board. A brass ring attached to the pulpit held the basin for baptisms and there was a nail for the preacher's hat.

Presbyterian ministers were educated men of good social standing. Jeremiah would have known the Reverend Michael Harrison who came to St Ives in 1706. During the years of persecution he had lived in Northamptonshire preaching in any available barn from a portable pulpit. During his time in St Ives the congregation grew to five hundred 'hearers' of whom forty were entitled to vote in Parliamentary elections. His congregation came from the town and surrounding villages. He died in 1721 and his will began with a ringing declaration *"In the name of God Amen. I, Michael Harrison of St Ives in the county of Huntingdon, clerk, being in good health and sound memory praised be God for it."* He asked that his wife should keep *"some books out of my study for her own reading and the rest or the major part of them to be sold."* Women were less likely to be literate than men. The next minister, the Reverend Josiah Hargrave, was friendly with widow Harrison. When she died in 1737 she left Mrs Hargrave her velvet hood and her daughter Rebecca *'my new silver spoon'*. Mr Hargrave must have been acceptable to the parish church officials as he baptised the young son of Richard Cordell in the parish church, an unusual occurrence.

The morning service began promptly with the singing of psalm 100 followed by a short but fervent prayer. A reading from the Old Testament came next, with a sermon based on the reading. The minister was expected to preach from the heart and not read his sermon. He then sang a psalm, prayed for thirty minutes, preached for another hour, prayed again, sang the 117th psalm and finally gave the blessing. Some found the services too plain and severe as ministers did not smile and cultivated a saintly manner. The congregation filed out afterwards, exchanged news and went home for a cold dinner. In the afternoon they returned for another service. This time Jeremiah and Ann accompanied the party. Mr Hargrave read and preached from the New Testament. Psalms from the Old Testament were sung in metrical form. The congregation had recently learnt one of the great hymns just published by Isaac Watts, 'When I survey the wondrous Cross'. The afternoon service only lasted two hours.

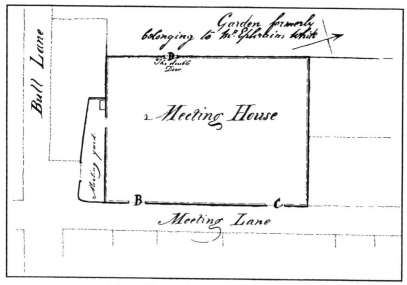

Plan of the Presbyterian Meeting House

After a supper of cold meat and pie, the family gathered to discuss the service. Jeremiah who had made notes led the discussion. His nephew was excused because he was young but Jeremiah remembered the occasions when his father had questioned him after the service to see what he had remembered. Woe betide him if he had dozed off or lost concentration! It would not have been unusual for his father to chastise him for his failure in answering correctly. His parents believed it was right to punish him for wrongdoing as it prevented him from going to Hell. Loving parents as they were they also felt guilt at giving the punishment. Jeremiah's generation was different. They did not believe in original sin and thought small children were innocent. They were more concerned to see that they behaved well so that they succeeded in their lives. Before they went to bed Jeremiah read a passage from the Bible and closed the day with prayers.

The observance of the Sabbath was strictly enforced by most people. Sunday was a day for peace and quiet without dancing or gaming. People were not allowed to sing at home or play a musical instrument. They did not travel or ride a horse on Sunday. Valentine Phipps of

Foxton was once charged that he was seen *'ridinge upon horseback on the Sunday towards St Ives market to buy Cattell'*. But in practice such rules did not apply to ordinary working people for whom Sunday was their day of recreation. *'They wandered out to the taverns and ale-houses and indulged in such sports as cock-fighting, bear- and bull-baiting or prize-fights.'* Amusements were forbidden on a Sunday; and were therefore held secretly for fear of an informer.

On this occasion the excitement of the fair had engulfed the town and one can imagine the young watching the arrival of jesters, tumblers and pedlars ready to sell all sorts of exciting items. Crowds milled around the Cross laughing and drinking before going home to prepare for the next day.

Whit Monday

Whit Monday was one of the busiest days of the year. Farmers came to the town to do business. Agricultural labourers and their families flocked in to enjoy their rare holiday and traders turned up to make money from visitors. St Ives was well prepared for this influx as it had around 200 'guest' beds and stabling for more than 400 horses. In addition to the visitors sleeping in the inns, many others used their rooms for business. There might be a lawyer meeting clients from the surrounding villages. Mr Charles Le Pla, an attorney, saw clients at St Ives and at the Black Bull in Cambridge on Saturdays. Traders hired rooms to auction goods, and merchants to purchase corn. Farmers might store grain in an inn or bring a sample to show a prospective buyer. Only the large farmers had grain to sell in May. The smaller farmer had been forced to sell his crop after the harvest at the best price he could get. He could not afford to wait for prices to rise as he needed the money to survive.

Drovers used inns for financial transactions as well as for eating and drinking. Because they brought cattle from a great distance, they were trusted to carry substantial sums of money for one another and were used as bankers. Perhaps Jeremiah knew of the court case in 1709 when the evidence was heard at the Cross Keys Inn in St Ives. The case was brought by one of two partners who had been acting together to buy and sell lean oxen. William Coates a "lean grasier" was from Pontefract in

Yorkshire and William Wright from Nottinghamshire. They were in dispute over the payment of £50 for the sale of some oxen. Coates said that at a meeting at Abbots Ripton an order was written out for him to pay the money in London to Mr Hanger of Abbots Ripton on the order of William Wright. When ten oxen were sold for the sum of £65, a bill of £50 was drawn on Mr Bennet in London (presumably a banker) for the benefit of Mr Wright and the rest paid in cash at St Ives. Subsequently there was a dispute as to whether the money had been received. At another meeting in Abbots Ripton Wright denied giving an order for the £50 to be paid to anyone else. A witness Richard Willis of Higham Ferrars declared that at a meeting in the Crown in St Ives the partners agreed that £50 should be paid to Wright but knew nothing about the money being paid to Mr Hanger on behalf of Mr Wright. Coates when challenged said that he had a receipt at home but if he could not find it he would pay the £50 from his own pocket. Unfortunately no-one knew what eventually happened.

As Jeremiah left the Unicorn, he saw that the Bullock Market was already set out with hurdles to hold pens of 10 or 20 cattle. He had often met the Scottish drovers who visited the market with their cattle on their way to Barnet and Smithfield. Some detoured into Norfolk to visit the fair outside Norwich and then took unsold cattle to St Ives or Essex. During the period when Irish cattle were being imported into England, Irish drovers also brought their cattle for sale in St Ives. The Scots would be driving in the famous black cattle from the *'cold and barren mountains of the Highlands'*. They were sold to fen farmers as *'guest cattle'* for fattening. The meat of the Scottish cattle was said to be *'so delicious for taste, that the inhabitants prefer 'em to the English cattle, which are much larger and fairer to look at.'* Cattle raised on local river meadows were also sold for fattening in the fens. After fattening they were driven to London for sale to butchers. Some drovers had spent the previous night to the north of St Ives at the little village of Broughton. Mounted on their tough little ponies they had set out very early that morning to drive their cattle or sheep into town. They sang or played an instrument to keep the cattle moving quietly forward. Other drovers had rented a close in St Ives for the night. This may have been why a small field in Pig Lane was called "Penny" close. They did not expect to sell all their animals in St Ives and pastured the rest of the herd before moving to another market the next day.

    Jeremiah's father had heard that early in the previous century innkeepers had bribed drovers to bring their cattle through their back gates and sell them privately either in their yard or in pens set up close to their houses to avoid paying tolls in the market. The innkeepers had undercut the official toll by charging the drovers four pence a pen for sheep and pigs. The Unicorn with its big yard had been ideal for this trade. But the duke's bailiff was left with the expense of setting up empty pens in the market and cleaning and repairing the surface afterwards. After a court case in 1636 the duke's right to receive tolls for the sale of livestock had been confirmed and all animals had to be sold in the market and the tolls paid to the bailiffs.

    We will assume that Jeremiah is interested in buying some Scottish cattle. He could buy animals direct from a farmer or in a market as at St Ives or Smithfield. Payment was made in stages. All parties had to provide credit until the butcher was able to pay the full price. If he did not want to buy direct he could use the services of a salesman who acted as the wholesaler for the trade. He advised the farmers when to sell to obtain a good price. When a retail butcher in Romford in Essex bought two bullocks from a local farmer, he promised to pay the salesman part of the cost on delivery, a further part at his market stall and the balance at Smithfield as soon as possible. A salesman might arrange with a farmer to find pasture for his sheep in Essex until they were sold and he would feed them until prices improved. *'These marshes were generally stocked (all the winter half year) with large fat sheep which they buy in Smithfield in September and October, when the Lincolnshire and Leicestershire graziers sell off their stock, and are kept here till Christmas, or Candlemas, or thereabouts, and though they are not made at all fatter here, than they were when bought in, yet the farmer, or butcher finds very good advantage in it, by the difference of the price of mutton between Michaelmas, when tis cheapest, and Candlemas when tis dearest; this is what the butchers value themselves upon, then they tell us at the market, that it is right marsh-mutton.'* We are talking about large numbers. 80,000 cattle and 610,000 sheep were sold at Smithfield market in any one year.

After Jeremiah had examined some cattle he walked to the market to look at some sheep. He might see the two men who were appointed each year to inspect the meat and fish on sale. One of these was a butcher and the other a waterman. It was important for the reputation of St Ives that the produce on sale was of good quality. There were two other officials who inspected leather for sale. They were normally cordwainers or shoemakers and curriers. These officials were appointed by the manorial court.

Jeremiah passed the Salutation Inn of his friend Thomas Swan and his immediate neighbour James Fisher the draper who lived in Godmanchester but was visiting St Ives today. Like all the buildings on the north side of the Sheep Market their properties stretched back to the lane called backside with an entrance for carts and horses. Visitors were thronging the yard to stable their horses and carts. The rooms in the inns were full of people eager to greet friends and complete their business.

Swan's near neighbour had been William Berriff a grocer who had died in 1727 leaving the property to his son William, who did not live in St Ives, on condition that he paid his mother ten pounds a year from the proceeds. A small amount of meadow was left to his daughter Elizabeth Crook. Because of his increasing old age William had managed the business with a partner called Jonathan Brittain who was also master of the workhouse. William Berriff's family had been haberdashers in St Ives in the seventeenth century. He, like his forebears, had been active in the administration of the St Ives. As a literate man he had been trusted to examine John Rowlett who had asked for a licence to set himself up as a schoolmaster.

William Berrife senior had produced his own coinage in the middle of the seventeenth century. At that time there was a grave shortage of small coins. As Pettis had written *'Grocers, innkeepers and almost any one stampt on copper or brass and made farthings and half pence. They were very light nor would pass any whear but near home.'*  Like others in St Ives he produced his own small coin with his name on one side and the sign of the Haberdashers Arms on the other. Officially such coinage ceased in 1672 with the production of copper half pence and farthings but in practice there were still many problems with money. *'King William the 3 call'd in all the old hamerd money of the silver coyn. For before this there was but little mill'd money, some little of Charles the 2 and a little of James the 2 and that mostly hoarded. The old being very bad it was handed about for nobody car'd to lett it ly by 'em and it got so ill a name that the women brou't out their hoarded old money and gave it to their husband or to a friend to dispose of it. Now that which was good silver was clipt, so the half crown was no bigger than a shilling and a shill than a six penc. And as for the base mettled money a half crown not worth a half penc, all other proportionable. Besids al this, there was abundanc of odd money, viz. one and twenty pieces, and 15 penc pieces, and thirteen and a half pieces and halfes of them and quarters. Four went for thirteen pence and a half penny but one alone for no more than three penc. Ther was nine peny pieces and four halfpence and grots with not ten grains which is but five farthings. Also three penny peics and two pence and one pence and a halfpence. Likewise Oliver Cromwell's coyn which some would take and some not. It ... was call'd the breeches money but I tho't by way of redicule. All which was troublesom to tell and difficult to take. Silver being thus, guinies advanc'd to thirty shillings curant, oft paid for more. Now in 1696 by Act of Parliament all hammard silver coyn was to be calld in and to be paid in to the King's tax and his other revenues by tolls to the 4 of May and afterward by weight at five shillings and two pence per ounce without any scrupel and a duty lay'd on windows for a term of years to make good the defficenci'.*

Next to William Berriffe were the premises of Edward Green, a tradesman wealthy enough to call himself a gentleman. His first wife had been the sister of the churchwarden Isaac Jones. John Green a cider merchant lived next door at the Sun, (Lloyds TSB). Beer and cider were the two most popular drinks of ordinary people and he expected to sell many flagons today. The inn had been called the Horseshoe earlier and included a bakery. Green was also a salesman. This meant that his trading activities covered all the important victuals of eighteenth century life, bread, meat and drink. Perhaps Jeremiah needed his help in his purchase of cattle and sheep and we will make him enter the Sun.

He looked first into the parlour which was furnished with a large oval table, a buffet stool and as many as twelve chairs with wooden seats. These were usually reserved for the master of the house or his important guests. As Green was not there Jeremiah looked into the attached Brick House which had a bigger room with one oval and three square tables. Here again there were wooden chairs and the room was beautifully decorated with six pictures. People were sitting and talking business in here but not with their host. He next tried the kitchen. Here Martha Green was supervising a busy scene. The dresser was piled high with pewter dishes and plates, next to it was the trencher rack for the many wooden trenchers or plates for less important guests. A roasting jack, suspended on its pulleys and weights, was gently turning a side of mutton before the fire. Two iron spits were used to cook chickens in front of a second fire. Pots and kettles were suspended over the grate and a small boy was using bellows to keep the fire at the right heat. The fire shovel, pokers and tongs were to hand. Martha Green was cooking the meat in a pan. She did not trust her servants to keep the fire at the right temperature or to turn the spit at the right speed. She knew that a ten pound piece of beef would cook in one and a half hours and six pounds of mutton in one hour *'at a quick fire'*. She was also entertaining her friends from neighbouring villages at the large oval table. On the wall hung her handsome looking glass, a comparative rarity in St Ives. John Green walked in from his yard and greeted Jeremiah. They went back into the yard to talk quietly about his business. As they walked Jeremiah could see the pantry with its salting tub to preserve meat, the brew house with its coppers for brewing and washing, the coal-house and the turf house. They agreed that Green would take charge of the beasts Jeremiah had purchased and deliver them in good condition to his shop in London.

Almost opposite John Green's house was the Town Pump and the eight stalls which the bailiffs had built in the open area of the market and which the inhabitants wanted removed as they restricted trade to the other side of the market. This part of the street was called Shoemakers' Row. It was an old name as there were no shoemakers working there.

The sign of the Bell Inn

Most of the buildings were inns. The first was called the Three Horseshoes, (Baker's Oven). James Nutter, a sievemaker and trustee of the Presbyterian meeting house, lived next door. His house was described as *'next the Three Horseshoes in the cornmarket'*. Corn, unlike cattle and sheep, could be sold privately in inns but there was also an open market. The local newspaper printed the prices of wheat, barley, rye, beans, peas and oats sold in the markets of St Ives, Huntingdon, St Neots, Peterborough, Newmarket, Cambridge, Bedford and London. London and Bedford prices were slightly higher than those in local markets. In St Neots the owner of the market was entitled to a toll on the sale of corn whether in the market or in shops, stalls, warehouses or boats. The toll was *'a dishfull conteyneing a quart out of a sacke conteineing foure bushells or thereabouts and four pence for every cartloade.'*

Nearby was the Bell, (Mackay's) with its unusual sign in the brick frontage. The Bell was owned by Mr Roger Thompson a brewer from Cambridge who also owned the Falcon on the opposite side of the market. He had inherited these inns from his grandfather. The townspeople thought of him as one of their own and celebrated when he was chosen to be a Justice of the Peace and High Sherriff for the counties of Huntingdonshire, Isle (of Ely) and Cambridgeshire for 1728. However his main home was at Rickmansworth in Hertfordshire and his visits to St Ives were infrequent. Then came the George, (Taylors Estate Agents and Size Up), and the Queens Arms, (Cadge) whose landlord was John Clark. His house had four chambers upstairs, one of which even had a hearth. It was unusual in St Ives to have heat in a bedroom. Clark had a small amount of meadow which he used for hay and to pasture his horse and a few sheep. Jeremiah knew that Elizabeth Clark had received an inheritance. They therefore had a few luxuries not generally seen in St Ives. In the Green Chamber there was a gun and a pair of window curtains as well as some escutcheons or shields with heraldic devices. The best chamber had the hearth as well as a looking glass, pictures and a clock, possibly made by Richard Enderby the local clockmaker. If it was a modern clock it would have two hands, instead of the more usual one hand for the hour.

The next inns were the Cross Keys (Peter Lane Estate Agents) and the Rose and Crown, (Barclays Bank) owned by Sir John Barnard. His steward looked after his interests as Sir John was a wealthy man who also owned the manors of Bury, Brampton and half of Hemingford Abbots. He was a Justice of the Peace and had been a Member of Parliament for Huntingdonshire. His family had conducted the negotiations when Henry Earl of Manchester was purchasing the manor of St Ives and Slepe in 1635. Jeremiah had seen a copy of a letter from Mr Robert Langley to Robert Barnard Esquire relating to this purchase. The Earl had paid £1406 for more than 114 tenements, all the agricultural land and the tolls of the market. As he would receive £91 each year in rent he recouped the cost of his purchase within fifteen years.

There were large numbers of sheep in pens in the sheep market. As many as 700 were regularly sold on a Monday. Some were bound to escape and the noise and smell must have been considerable. At this point Jeremiah met his farmer friend John Cordel and was invited to visit him the next day. At this point we will imagine him leaving the noise and crush to turn down White Hart lane to visit Sir Edward Lawrence at St Ives Hall. Horses were for sale in this lane with men running them up and down to prove that they were in sound health and wind. On his left was Padlemore, an enclosed area with fruit trees and two houses one of which was the Pipe House where clay pipes for smoking were manufactured.

It was here that the great fire of St Ives had started in 1689, in a malt house in Whitehart Lane next door to Padlemore.

'Tusday april 30 Hear happened a Sudden & dreadfull fire In a Malt house at the Whithart Lane next padlemore. The wind being very high it ran up to the Stret flew cross the Sheep market consuming all to the reverside with part of the Bridg Street & to the other side the bridge consum'd part of them two Houses.

It laid in ashes several Inns Messuages & dwelling Houses belonging to 122 persons & families togather with Household good Malt Corn Grain Hay Shopgoods wares & Marchantdizes

The damage amounting to Upwards of £13,072. Came in by Voluntary contribution towards this loss 2066.11.4½d Collected by Breeiff 1478.5.10 ½, in all 3544.17.3d.'

The fire damaged several cottages in the lane, together with the White Hart and its neighbour, some houses near the present Town Hall and two buildings on the other side of the river. In other buildings like the Cross Keys Inn, (the present office of the Gateway Building Society), a huge beam still shows signs of scorching on the north side.

Opposite Paddlemore was St Ives Hall where Sir Edward Lawrence lived when he was in the town. (It is now the site of Cromwell Place). The house stood on its own, surrounded by small fields called closes. It had a grand circular drive to the front, which led into a courtyard. The house itself was not particularly large. There were three storeys with three sets of large chimneys. Inside was a lovely staircase much admired. Behind it was another courtyard with buildings to north and south. Then there were spacious gardens with a circular pond leading to a formal arrangement of flower beds. They were laid out in a triangular pattern, perhaps with box hedges and grass and a tree in each segment. There was a water feature on the south side similar to one at Burleigh House at Stamford. This was the only formal garden in St Ives which accentuated the difference between Sir Edward and the rest of the townspeople.

It was nonetheless an old fashioned style of gardening. In the seventeenth century the formal gardens of France had been much admired and imitated. Under King William III, Dutch gardens became popular

ST IVES HALL.
Plan taken from Pettis' map
After engraving Norris Museum

with '*all kinds of figures cut in box, of which I have never seen so large a quantity, and of such uncommon height*'. Lawrence's garden was of this kind, heavy on geometry, with straight symmetrical paths, level ground, clipped hedges and shaped trees. Fences divided the garden from the fields to keep cattle out . It was extremely expensive on labour. By 1713 fashionable writers begged people to stop moulding their trees into '*cones, globes and Pyramids*'. They suggested that land should retain its natural shape, with irregular paths and hillocks with trees 'to imitate Nature more'. A garden should also grow fruit and vegetables.

If Sir Edward Lawrence were at home that weekend he would be expected to offer hospitality. '*This is the day of our fair*' sulked Sir Joseph Banks in 1753, '*when according to immemorial custom I am to feed and make drunk everyone who chooses to come, which will cost me in beef and ale near £20.*' There is no record of the attitude of the Lawrence family to the townsfolk but we will assume that he followed this tradition. As Jeremiah may have supplied Sir Edward with meat in London it would be important to pay him a visit. The gentry gave a tradesman money, perhaps £100, and then ordered meat until the money was spent. They were notorious for not paying tradesmen until compelled by threats of the bailiffs. Whether he was owed money or not it would be to his advantage to call on the Squire.

Jeremiah entered the hall of the house and stood in line to greet Sir Edward who was dressed to impress his visitors. The social gulf between them was enormous. The guests were seated at a large table and plied with beer and beef while Sir Edward sat at a second table away from the throng. His sister Elizabeth was acting as hostess helped by her husband Josiah Woollaston. Her son Isaac was his uncle's heir. Mistress Woollaston was wearing a large silk hoop skirt. Panniers made from osier reeds into the shape of a basket were strapped on each hip and the many yards of fabric of the skirt draped over them. She sat on a chair without arms to allow for the width of her skirt. In contrast to such an elaborate dress her hair was dressed close to her head and covered with a dainty lace cap.

Sir Edward was unmarried. He had been a gentleman usher to Queen Anne as a young man and Member of Parliament for Stockbridge for five years. After that he had given up politics. He was currently serving as a Justice of the Peace. He also performed his duty as a juror at the Assizes and attended the annual vestry meeting at the parish church. He was the largest landowner in St Ives owning five hundred acres of land, more than a quarter of the total acreage. Half of his land was freehold in large blocks in the common fields. The other half was copyhold and divided into strips. This was rented by tenants. There were therefore many people depending on him for their livelihood.

Oliver Cromwell had been his tenant for five years in the middle of the seventeenth century before he inherited his own estate in Ely. While in St Ives he was fined by the manorial court for allowing his shepherd to put too many animals on the common. Jeremiah did not know what lands he had farmed but he had heard that he rented Green End Farm and its sixteenth barn from the Lawrence family. This was now called Cromwell's barn. Cromwell was important enough to attend the vestry meeting at the parish church and to sign the register. Although as a Puritan he led worship in private houses he also attended the parish church. There were tales that he used to wrap his neck in red flannel because of problems with his throat.

Cromwell's Barn

Jeremiah knew that Sir Edward Lawrence was often absent from St Ives and that he had upset some people. He had objected to something written in the local newspaper, the St Ives Post Boy. A *'Mr John Fisher erected a Printing office hear for Books News etc who by ill manigment fail'd his press in Ted's Lane. Mr Robt Rakes succeeded and sett up his press in Fish Street.'* One of Raikes' advertisements was as follows "*A consolatory epistle to the Jocks of Great Britain* " sold at the printing office in St Ives and by the men that carry the news of whom also any person may be furnished with all sorts of double and single maps, large and small copper prints ... likewise all sorts of playhouse songs (with the notes best for the Voice and Flute), fine Dutch writing paper for 7d a Quire." Raikes's business prospered and he *'took Mr Wm Dicey in partner with him & went on well but chanced to bring something that did not suit the times nor pleas a certain Knight who brou't him under prosecution & fine. Soon after Left the Town Mr Rakes to Gloster, Mr Dicey to Norhamton and there set up their severall Presses.'* The gossip was that both Raikes and Dicey were very successful with their newspapers in Gloucester and Northampton.

Sir Edward Lawrence as a Justice of the Peace had wide and largely unsupervised powers. He could issue warrants for arrest, punish offenders for drunkenness, vagrancy or swearing and had the power to commit suspects for trial at the assizes. He expected to use these powers if there was any trouble at the fair. Two justices could decide whether to licence an alehouse, decide on the paternity of a baby or deal with a runaway servant or apprentice. A common problem was poaching. Henry Lee of Houghton was charged with *'feloniously stealing, killing and carrying away one sheep out of the grounds called How Hills of the goods and chattells of Symon.'* Martin was renting this land from Sir Edward. Justices also fixed wages and prices, organised apprenticeships, swore in the constables, ordered improvements to highways and to drains. They licensed fairs like today's and administered the poor law. They were unpaid and expected to spend many hours on all these duties. As a major landowner and Justice Sir Edward was in such a powerful position that townspeople looked at him with respect and fear.

Mr Robert Piggott who owned the Priory might have ridden over for the day from his home at Connington in Cambridgeshire. He had recently been elected one of the two Members of Parliament for the county when a previous member, the Marquis of Hartington, a cousin of the first Duke of Montagu, became the Duke of Devonshire. Sometimes a candidate was returned unopposed. If there was a contest, bribery, intimidation, and fraud were common. In order to qualify electors must own land valued at forty shillings or more a year. Candidates wooed local voters with cash, trinkets, public entertainments, speeches, flattery, and open house. *"Your doors are open to every dirty fellow in the county that is worth forty shillings a year; all my best floors are spoiled by the hobnails of farmers stamping about them; every room is a pig-stye, and the Chinese paper in the drawing room stinks so abominably of punch and tobacco that it would strike you down to come into it.'* Voters were bullied by sermons in church or even by the threat of mob violence.

Under the first two Georges, Tories were excluded from office. But the costs of permanent exclusion from office were so damaging that, from the late 1720s, a trickle of Tories cut their losses and came in from the cold, deserting to the Whig and Court party. Although the four members of Parliament for Huntingdonshire were Tories they all supported the Whig first minister Sir Robert Walpole. He owed his success as first minister to the support of local gentry. They saw him as one of their own. He enjoyed the same kind of country pursuits and spoke with a Norfolk accent. Country squires liked the plainness of his speech and manners and were suspicious of the affectation of courtiers. *"They took their pleasures in decent, measured ways; in the quiet delights of a clay pipe or plum pudding, drowsing through a sermon, tickling a trout, strolling with the family or paying calls on a Sunday, practising self-improvement, singing in a catch-club, or cultivating one's garden"*. Walpole's government was assisted by the relative prosperity of these years. The trade balance was favourable and agriculture, industry and commerce were all doing well. Food prices were low so that famine was unlikely and the population was growing slowly.

Landowners however disliked the land tax which they felt was an unfair burden on their class. Walpole had won popularity by gradually reducing the rate since 1728 and it was rumoured that he was considering imposing a tax on salt as an alternative. But opposition to this move was growing in London and the country. Shopkeepers and traders accused Walpole of grinding the faces of the poor to aid wealthy landowners. Traders were most unhappy at the thought of giving more power to excise officers to search their premises for untaxed salt. It was an attack on the privacy of an Englishman and they preferred to have nothing to do with excise officers. Another visitor to St Ives Hall was the vicar. He considered himself a member of the gentry and needed to pay particular attention to the wishes of his patron Robert Piggott.

After dinner, the gentry walked down to the fair. They felt it their duty to patronise local retailers and potential voters. '*The proudest Englishman will converse familiarly with the meanest of his countrymen; he will take part in their rejoicings. At election time it is not uncommon to see the lowest of citizens receiving letters from the most illustrious candidates, in which, in the most polite terms possible, they solicit the favour of their votes.*'

They walked to the corner of the White Hart inn whose tenant was Richard Allen. The terms of his lease required that he paid an annuity of twelve pounds per annum to Dorothy Fisher, a relative of the owner. In 1693 George Nutter had purchased the cottage next door which was described as part of '*the land where the White Hart stood.*' This was four years after the fire when the house had been completely demolished. Now it was rebuilt and rented to six families of whom John Butler was well-known as he had lost two wives both within a few years of marriage. Another tenant was the baker John Martin who sold a special dough sweetened with sugar and flavoured with spices at fair time. This was a special treat on high days and holidays.

Next to the baker lived a milkman, John Gee who was a cousin of Jeremiah's. His grandfather Obediah Gee had applied for a licence for his house as the first Presbyterian meeting house in 1672. Finally there was the small cottage of John Hemington just before the workhouse at the end of the market. Perhaps some of the inhabitants were sitting on a bench in the sun enjoying the sights. The aim of the workhouse was "*to grind rogues honest, and idle men industrious*". In practice most inmates were either very young and or very old, the chronic sick, rogues, vagrants and village simpletons.

After the sale of animals the fair proper started. Saturday and Sunday had seen the arrival of peddlers and hawkers with their trains of thirty or forty animals, the leader wearing a bell to warn other packhorse owners. England was notoriously '*hell for horses*' and work-animals were driven relentlessly. Hawkers had to pay a fee to the government for the right to travel around the country selling goods. They mostly sold cloth, ribbons and similar items. Peddlers did not need a licence as they sold untaxed items like printed papers and food. Then there were travelling tinkers who sold small metal items or would offer to mend a broken pan. A big fair attracted them all. It was an opportunity for local people to buy goods not normally available and to enjoy the entertainment on offer. There were crowds of people who had streamed into the town, on horseback, by boat, in carts or on foot. They had left their villages before day-break and were in a festive mood.

When they arrived they found that the town was laid out to tempt their pennies from their purses. At Sturbridge Fair in the autumn in Cambridge, in addition to the trading in livestock and tools, there were for sale '*all sorts of wrought iron, and brass ware from Birmingham; edged tools, knives etc from Sheffield; glass ware, and stockings, from Nottingham, and Leicester; and an infinite throng of other things of smaller value.*' In St Ives there were also the stalls of resident shopkeepers set out in front of their premises. The shoemaker in the Bullock Market expected custom as well as the tinplate workers in Bridge Street. Edmund Pettis had put his goods for sale on the pavement in front of his premises. As a cooper by trade he sold barrels and wooden items like spade handles. Thomas Dillingham had come from Ramsey to sell his rush mats. Farmers' wives came in from the country to sell their butter, cheese and bacon. Merchants had already been round the stalls buying up the butter which was marketed through Cambridge and sent to London salted in tubs. Most of their cheese was usually sold at the Michaelmas fair.

The Selbys who lived near the parish church had a stall in the market for their confectionery. A universal treat at fairs were sugar-coated nuts, gingerbread or buns flavoured with spices and fruit. These were sold at stalls like that of the Selby's or cried through the streets. They sold gingerbreads in the shape of letters to help children learn the alphabet.

Thomas and Sarah Selby in their youth had been witnesses in the ecclesiastical courts. Sarah had been '*standing at her stall sometime in the afternoone and did hear Alice Carter in a very violent and rude manner and without any provocation in the publick open markett and before a great number of people which hath gather'd together say unto John Ibbott, junior, severall times these words or words to this effect following "You are a Rogue*

and have a care you are not arraigned at the barr as your father was." This referred to his father Bartholomew Ibbott a Quaker. His son felt insulted and laid a complaint against Alice Carter. The case was heard in the parish church in Huntingdon. Three years later the Selbys were back in the same courts for defaming Edward Revell, another Quaker. They were witnesses for a third time in a case of defamation between Robert Sisson and Sarah Sharpe. This time Thomas Selby gave evidence. The case concerned *'a difference between Robert Sisson and his wife and an uproar or hubbub happening in the Strete and against the doore of the said Robert Sisson. Sarah Sharpe was amongst the crowd and Robert frequently in his passion walking to and agen in his entry and comeing to his streete doore Sarah did for several times call Robert a rogue saying to him "You are a rogue, you beate and abuse your wife."* She then said to another neighbour that *"Neighbour Sisson is a sorry man for he would have raked my daughter."* Selby gave evidence that on another occasion *'he was standing at his own door talking with Robert Sisson'* who had seen Sarah Sharpe coming and said to Selby *"Yonder comes one of my adversaries."* He called out to Sarah *"Are you not a rare woman to make all this disturbance and abuse me after the rate you have done?"* To which Sarah replyed *"I have not abused you. I have neither medled nor made with you that I know off."* To which Robert replyed *"You are a Lyar, hussey and I will make you known. You have said that I would have ravished your daughter."* Sarah replied *"Noe, I doe not say soe but you are a pittifull dog or Rogue and would have raked her."* Such excitement meant that people in the town might be wary of the Selbys.

Jeremiah wanted to visit George Barton of Huntingdon. He opened his shops in Peterborough, St Ives and St Neots every market day where he bought and sold books, maps, paper, cards, snuff and snuff boxes. Second-hand books could always be picked up from stalls and peddlers. When Benjamin Franklin the great American was in London in

1724 he hung around the bookstalls, picking up a book and reading for as long as he decently could. Milton called them "stallreaders". They wandered round London from stall to stall, reading a little here, a little there, and even turning down the page of a book so that they could return to it. It was not only the gentry who could read. Nursery rhymes taught home truths to toddlers and helped the young to learn to count; decks of cards taught the ABC and numbers, and shop and tavern signs and church interiors familiarized people with words and their associations. Jeremiah remembered the poor weaver Nathan Neave whose only major possession was his Bible. Even some of the poorest people who could not read told each other stories from the Bible and they in turn repeated them word for word. A foreigner travelling in England described a woman selling herbs at her stall who was reading a little book on the monuments in Westminster Abbey. He *"conversed with several people of the lower class who all knew their national authors, and who all have read many if not all of them"*. On the other hand he also tells how he travelled by coach with three farmers, none of whom could read or write. Ballad singers were very popular and sometimes adapted their songs to tell scurrilous stories about local people. The news of Thomas Swan's adultery was broadcast by means of ballads circulated in Cambridge and the surrounding villages.

There were fishwives with their baskets on their heads selling oysters, boiled whelks, mussels or pickled herrings. They paraded through the town calling out their wares and trying to drown out the opposition with their cries. Barrow boys took round seasonal fruit and vegetables. Others sold sheeps' trotters and black puddings. There were girls selling spring flowers. Some were trying to sell old clothes and hats. These might have been stolen or forfeited from an innkeeper like the Horners when a debt was not repaid. Louder still was the voice of the Town Cryer. He was paid one shilling for crying anything lost or found, or for posting bills, or for crying sales by auction or for crying any animal put in the pound. Today he had various cries. A horse had strayed from a farmyard and the owner was offering one guinea for its safe return. Twins of two years old had been left at Needingworth. The Overseers of the Poor were offering a reward of £5 for information about the mother. Two apprentices had run away. Thomas Phillips was apprenticed to Thomas Peacock of Spaldwick a blacksmith and Matthew Ruff to William Nicholls a weaver of Great Raveley. People were warned that the two boys must be returned to their masters and should not be harboured. Finally he had a more cheerful cry that *'A gentleman had recently arrived to teach rapier or small-sword. He may be spoken with at the Crown any day in the week.'*

Bakers sent out their apprentices with baskets of apple pies or gingerbread and butchers with home-make sausages. They stood at street corners crying their hot and cold viands. Retailers had to work hard at selling. They could not rely on customers calling at their shops. Customers needed to be careful with their purchases. All goods were hand-made, the quality varied and there were no refrigerators. By the end of the day goods were much cheaper and the very poor might be able to make some purchases. They were more likely to buy bad or mouldy food.

The gentry might walk around with small coins in their pockets to give to beggars. A fair was an occasion when the rich and poor mingled together and a wealthy man was expected to show some generosity. They enjoyed the organs, fiddles and tambourines of a travelling mountebank performing in the streets hoping to be paid for the entertainment. There might be groups of travelling players. Some were half entertainers and half quack-doctors, who set up their booths in the market places of country towns. One used to arrive in a coach drawn by men in uniform. *"Footmen in yellow were his tumblers and trumpeters, those in blue his merry-andrew, his apothecary and spokesman. He was dressed in velvet and had in his coach a woman who danced upon the ropes."* Such people were very popular. They provided entertainment like tight-rope dancing, tumbling and various acrobatic feats. They also sold powders, pills and ointments, which they assured their audiences had already cured half the crowned heads of Europe. Some even produced certificates, medals and large seals, which they said had been bestowed upon them by grateful princes. Festivals like the Whitsun fair allowed children to scrounge cakes and half-pennies, and let off steam for once in a while. The day was celebrated with feasting, with music and with dancing.

Any market and fair attracted its fair share of petty crime and the constables expected to be busy. Sometimes the cry of "Stop thief" was heard. John Lovel of Ramsey, a visitor to St Ives, was robbed at the market. But because the constables did not arrest anyone for this offence the Justices held the town responsible and charged it more than nine pounds to recompense the victim. Another common crime was the pretty, nicely dressed miss who persuaded a man to have a drink and then disappeared with his purse. As the evening wore on the constables expected to have to deal with drunks. If they became too difficult they were escorted to the tollbooth and locked up. Richard Skeeles, from Chatteris, had been brought in front of the Justice, Richard Drury. He had attacked the constable Joseph Child and *'sware and cursed the Justice as he did his duty and shouted "God damn the Bible".* He would be dealt with later. They had already locked up Robert Asdell who was frequently drunk. For many years he had held a grudge against the excise officers, having accused one of them Obediah Patrick of cheating. When he had been drunk in the publick house of Robert Knightley, *'in a room next the street'* he had said that *"If any man lived ten year longer they would see that rogue Patrick hanged for he robbed me and cheated the Queen"*. John Mortimer was one of the witnesses who heard him saying this. *"He had gone into the kitchen to light his pipe and was returning to the room next the street when he heard him say the words."* Mortimer himself was called by Asdell "*a setting dog*". It did not help Asdell's temper that he lost the case.

The constables had originally been appointed by the manorial court but were now chosen by the vestry. For some of their duties they came under the authority of the local Justice of the Peace. In general, constables served for one year and were elected in rotation from farmers and craftsmen. There were three in St Ives, one chosen for the Green and two for the Street. The Street included most of the Broadway, Bridge Street and the Sheepmarket, the urban area. The Green covered the houses around the parish church and the agricultural parts of the parish. Like all the other parish officials, constables were unpaid and no expenses were given for loss of earnings. Daniel Defoe wrote that the office of constable was one of '*unsupportable hardship... it takes up so much of a man's time that his own affairs are frequently totally neglected, too often to his ruin.*' However, it was also an honour which gave the holder status in the town.

The constables were responsible for law and order. They had to keep the stocks, pillory and lock-up in good order. They saw to it that vagrants were whipped and offenders were arrested and escorted to the assizes. If a thief was caught he or she would be held in prison in Huntingdon until the time of the Assizes. The most severe sentence was transportation. Alternatively the felon was pilloried. The pillory was a wooden frame that fitted over the head and hands. The felon was often tormented by the crowd and pelted with food, dirt, dead animals or even stones. Branding was an alternative punishment or a public flogging, particularly popular if the victim was a prostitute. When the safety of the nation was threatened, the constables could be instructed to raise the local militia. Finally constables were responsible for the accuracy of weights and measures and the supervision of alehouses.

After the gentry had enjoyed the entertainment they turned down the lane to the Priory (now called Market Lane). They wanted to avoid the workhouse and the lane near the Priory barn because of the mess left by the pigs which had been sold by its wall. At least it was May and there were no ducks on sale. In the autumn and winter fenmen brought in the wildfowl for sale. They had been caught in '*duckoys, places so adapted for the harbour and shelter of wild-fowl, and then furnished with a breed of those they call decoy-ducks, who are taught to allure and entice their kind to the places they belong to, that it is incredible what quantities of wild-fowl of all sorts, duck, mallard, teal, widgeon, etc they take in those duckoys every week, during the season.'* The ducks were taken to St Ives and then brought up to London; *'they generally sent up three thousand couple a week.'* May was the breeding season and so none were for sale. Butchers like Jeremiah did not sell poultry and fowl. These were the speciality of poulterers, a separate trade.

The Priory was considerably smaller than St Ives Hall. It was approached from the west side through an orchard. The drive led up to the front of the house and there were fields behind it. In one of them was a large well of sweet water with walls made of roughly hewn stone. Behind the Priory was the medieval barn, once the property of the monks from Ramsey. It was still used to store tithes of corn.

As the guests entered the house Jeremiah started to walk back to the Unicorn along the south side of the market. He recognised the cottage of the shoemaker by the sign of a boot hanging over the doorway. The best shoes were made to order but the poor had to buy them ready made. It was much better to have shoes made to fit. When two shoemakers died in the seventeenth century their stock included ready made shoes and boots as well as *'13 dozen 6 pair of children's shoes in white, yellow and red'*. They also had leather for soles and uppers, lasts, wooden heels, hammers, trees and dressed hides.

Another cottage was owned by William Rolls, a whitesmith, who worked in tin and iron. His wife was a very capable woman who helped run the workshop when William was out selling goods or buying materials. Their neighbour was John Wadmore a relative of Jeremiah's sister who was pleased to see him. The bigger properties near the centre of the town were more inns. There was the Angel of Edward Hoddy who had recently died leaving his property to his brother Richard of St Neots to pay for *'meat, drink and apparell'* for his four year old son Ebenezer. When he reached fourteen Edward wanted his brother to apprentice Ebenezer for seven years to William Edmund *'who is related to my wife or to Matthew Selby both being shoemakers'*. In the event of the boy's death the brother would inherit the estate. He was to use the cash from the sale of *'the moveables'* to pay off part of the mortgate to Mr Nutter. In the meantime the Angel was being run by Robert Audley, who also worked as a porter on the quay.

Jeremiah noticed that the inn next to the Angel had a sign newly painted showing one swan. The last time he had been in St Ives the sign had three swans painted on it and when he was a boy he had known it as the White Swan. (It is now known as the Robin Hood). It was once owned by an Archbishop of Canterbury. Other inns were the Cock which had been 'consumed by fire' in 1689, the Red Lion, now called the Golden Lion and the Skinners Arms. This was the start of the area known as the Butchers' Shambles, the site of the Free Church. The houses faced the stalls which had encroached on the area of the market. There were four butchers' shops including one rented to Thomas Jackson with its slaughterhouse, yard and four acres of meadow. Customers recognised butchers by their distinctive aprons and the area by its smells, flies and vermin. Nothing was so disgusting as butchers' shops. The better ones had a slaughterhouse behind them but others used the street and adjacent lanes to kill and butcher the animals. The fresh meat was sold on the stalls and the entrails were bought in the side lanes. Some of this was fed to pigs. Butchers tried to keep their premises clean by throwing the waste into tubs and disposing of it at night in the river.

Beyond the Shambles Jeremiah recognised the sign of the Falcon, whose landlord, William Christmas, he had known in the old days. His inn had four rooms on the ground floor, a kitchen, brewhouse, hall and little room, in addition to the cellar and yard and outhouses. He kept pigs in the yard and fed them scraps from the inn or from the Shambles. On the first floor were four chambers well furnished with beds, chairs, chest of drawers and hanging press (cupboard). The neighbouring property was a cottage which backed on to Robert Lancaster's house in Bridge Street. There were two other small cottages that ran along the south side of Crown Street before the Red Bull on the corner (New Look), facing the Red Cow on the other side of Bridge Street.

Perhaps in a less crowded part of the street he might see a coin lying on the ground and would remember his father's story about James Atkins a tailor from Swavesey who had visited St Ives market. He had seen a similar groat but before he could pick it up a stranger, Elisha Kelleman, bent down and grabbed the coin. He asked if Atkins '*would go with him to the sign of the Crowne in St Ives and take part of the said money; which he accepted and went into a chamber at ye said inn, where was also one William Booles, who producing a pack of cards went to play with Atkins, where they cheated him of his goods to the value of twelve shillings, and in money to the value of two shillings.'* However Atkins was brave enough to admit that he had been fooled and had the two men arrested. They had to remain in Huntingdon gaol until the time of the Assizes and were fined five shillings because of the time they had already spent in gaol.

In these quieter lanes Jeremiah might be accosted by girls. *'About nightfall they range themselves in a file in the foot-paths of all the great streets, in companies of five or six, most of them dressed very genteelly. The low taverns serve them as a retreat, to receive their gallants in; in those houses there is always a room set apart for this purpose. Whole rows of them accost passengers in the broad day-light.'* We will assume that Jeremiah hurries past them ignoring their calls.

On his way home he stopped to watch cock-fighting on the Waits. This was a very popular attraction which drew large crowds. The fights were seen as manly trials of skill and courage. A labourer trained a bird to fight hoping to make his fortune. Betting was common and the shouts and swearing could be heard at some distance.

As daylight faded visitors thought about returning home. Others were remaining for the night, sleeping in inns or alehouses. Back at the Unicorn Jeremiah found a busy scene. Fairs were celebrated with feasting and dancing. Such feasts were described by one writer as *'swilling and gulling, night and day, till they be as drunke as Apes, and as blockish as beasts.'* The kitchens were a hive of activity. Ann was helping to serve the customers thronging all the downstairs rooms. As night fell bonfires were lit and fireworks exploded. Young couples slipped away into the darkness. It was their night for enjoyment.

Their Final Day

It was their last day. They had been invited to go with brother Joseph to see the ceremony of Bible Dicing, the last celebration of the Whitsun weekend. But before that they had to make an important call. They needed to talk with John Reynolds who was buying the Unicorn. They walked together through the Unicorn yard into Ted's Lane and then along Willow Row and Cank Alley to Cold Harbour (near the North Road carpark) where John Reynolds, the blacksmith, lived in one of the bigger houses in this part of St Ives. Reynolds told them that although he had purchased the inn he had not yet been able to register the sale in the manorial court. He needed proof that the loans on the property had been paid off before the transfer could be registered. Jeremiah agreed to provide the necessary documents. They next went to Joseph's cottage with its granary and stable in Ted's Lane. He rented it from John Noble a cordwainer at an annual rental of £3. Joseph's father-in-law, a carpenter, lived around the corner in a cottage in Pig Lane. His was the last house on the edge of the town. Joseph's wife was spinning flax. They needed a new bed (what is now called a mattress). Once she had spun the flax she would take it to a weaver who would make up the cloth. She would then stitch the sides together to form the bed and stuff it with goose and duck feathers.

Many poorer people lived in this part of the town. It was a lively area crammed with small overcrowded cottages. They were often one-room hovels, flimsy wooden structures with a beaten earth floor. Without

a well some were forced to buy water from itinerant sellers. Labourers rose with the dawn and went to bed when night fell. Candles were an expensive luxury. *"Humanity shudders at the idea of the industrious labourer, with a wife and five or six children, being obliged to live or rather to exist, in a wretched, damp, gloomy room, of 10 or 12 ft square, and that room without a floor.'* The most popular house was the Fleur de Lys which belonged to John Skinner. On such a day it was full of drinkers as many weavers and shoemakers were still celebrating Whitsun. They were discussing the cockfights of the previous day as their host owned the cockpit on the Waits.

As they walked along, Jeremiah pointed out to Ann the official paupers of the town. A few years ago the vestry meeting had decided that *'all persons who shall be clothed by the parish with outward garments shall be clothed in blue jersey and have a square piece cut out of the sleeve and a badge set in the same place.'* Paupers were identified and stigmatised by this and were refused the dole if they did not wear the uniform.

Although people boasted of the roast beef of Old England, the poor were in fact obliged to fill themselves up with bread because the price of beef was too high. Even a family of four children with a father in skilled work might only be able to buy fat bacon once a week. If they could afford to buy tea, they used the leaves over and over again. Even so, they probably ate white bread and looked with horror at the rye and barley bread of their ancestors. This diet was so low in protein that many of the poor were weakened by rickets and scurvy. The minimum income for survival was about £20 a year and perhaps as many as twenty per cent of the population were below that level and needed assistance.

There was a life cycle of poverty among the labouring classes. When a man married and had a young family his wife could not work which reduced the family income. If he fell sick or died, his wife and children were forced to go to the parish for relief. It might allow them a small pittance or send them to the workhouse. Overseers could make small payments for house repairs, funerals, clothes, tools or medicine. Small sums were paid if local people could not work because of temporary hardship as their labour would be needed when the economy improved. Shoemakers could not work in the depths of a cold winter as the waxed threads they used to sew shoes froze. Then they would be laid off as they were paid by the piece. This must have happened when the river froze in 1683. *'November 17 Saturday set in a great Frost & froz Night & day so seavear that working ceased for some time till peoples bodys ware season'd unto it. Then went on again yet Still it continued to an Extream Not abundanc of Snow nor much wind But thick rimes for many days & nights Continuanc some times clear for a great while with a very sevear keen air Thus it contin'd to the 23 of Decr. When it thaw'd a little which gave hopes twas going but prov'd a mistake. For it Freez againe as Vemant as ever Twas very troublesom to presarve any bear And as hard to gett water for Cattel All ponds brooks & Rivers being lock't so fast that loaden cartes could go almost any whear Thus it continu'd with little or no abatement tell the 20 of Feby when it began to thaw gradual & without much rain'* Floods would have a similarly disastrous effect. In 1725 many families had needed help from the overseers until the floods subsided and they could work again.

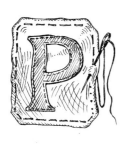

When people were too old to work the parish could pay their rent, put them in a small cottage owned by the parish or board them with a more active neighbour.

Three people had left money in their wills to endow charities to assist the poor. On Ash Wednesday a sermon was preached and bread distributed to poor widows in memory of Mr Thomas Sharp. The same happened on Good Friday, this time in memory of his sister, Mrs Elizabeth Sharp. A third charity of Mr Langley was distributed to widows and children in January. In one year fifty four persons received gifts of whom thirty seven were widows.

Overseers had to propose a rate each year to maintain the poor of the town. The Easter parish meeting decided on the number and size of pensions for the elderly and the overseers handed out the doles to those suffering temporary hardship. This meant that they had to appeal directly to them for aid that was either granted or refused. In addition to helping those unable to work, the overseers arranged for the board and lodging of orphans. Money was given perhaps to a widow to pay for their clothes, food, rent, and fuel. The food was barely above subsistence level, but probably much the same as for those in work. When the orphans were old enough the overseers apprenticed them to local householders. This was not always an easy task. Those who took on such apprentices signed an indemnity to the parish of St Ives that they would not make any charge on the parish until the term of the apprenticeship was completed. Henry Dean, a victualler, agreed to these terms for his apprentice Jane Johnson until she reached the age of twenty-one. The officers of Hemingford Grey paid St Ives two pounds as indemnity for 'Old Pen's boy' and the same for 'Hill's boy'. A widow called Mary Eaton had taken on the care of a child. When she was dying she left everything to her brother on condition that he took *'care of the child I am intrusted with by the Parish.'* As she owned two cows and some hay she left sufficient to pay for his keep.

The overseers were also paid to be suspicious of newcomers to the town. It was their task to decide whether such people would become a burden on the rates. If they did not belong to the town the overseers could apply for a certificate from a local Justice of the Peace to remove them to the parish in which they were legally settled. This was likely to happen if the newcomer looked poor or if a woman was heavily pregnant. It was the duty of the overseers to drive the unfortunate woman away into the next parish. If the baby was born in the town it had the right of settlement and therefore the mother could remain. For example, the natural daughter of Mary Broffitt had been baptised recently. As an unmarried mother, Mary might have been forced to stand dressed in a white sheet in the church porch as a penance for her sin of having a child outside marriage. Nonetheless she and the child had the right to live in the town and be supported when they needed help. Conversely when a painter from Cambridge wanted to marry a pauper Catherine Stimpson the overseers were pleased to pay him three pounds three shillings for a dinner and for the marrying and the remainder for himself. He was paid in effect to take her away from the parish. Foreman Biggs had relations in trade in St Neots, so the overseer signed a settlement certificate for him, his wife Elizabeth and their three children to live there. St Ives however remained responsible for their welfare if necessary. It happened in reverse. Justices in St Neots had recently granted their overseers an order to remove to St Ives James Mayes and his wife Elizabeth with their new born daughter Ann. Outsiders could settle if they possessed a certificate from their original parish and could demonstrate that they were able to support themselves. John Cropper, a trustee of the Baptist Church, had originally come from Whittlesey with a correct certificate. He had no problem in settling in St Ives because he bought a property. Poorer people could settle if they were contracted as servants for a year or if they were an apprentice or the tenant of a house. Those who were destitute because of unemployment, illness or incapacity were driven away.

It had been the turn of Mr Gilbert Cordell and Mr James Morton to be the overseers of the poor for the previous year. If either had refused to serve he could be fined by the Justices. The job was unpaid and involved making difficult and sometimes unpleasant decisions but carried a certain amount of prestige as only substantial householders were called upon to serve in this office. Overseers were assisted by two people. Charles Eaton, the parish clerk, was paid forty shillings a year to register the rates for the poor and to pay the bills and John Martin received five pounds a year for his duties as a paid overseer. He did many of the daily tasks under the supervision of the elected officers. His was a controversial appointment. At the vestry meeting at Easter a motion had been tabled *"Is John Martin a fit person to serve any office in the parish in the future?"* After a vote it was decided that he should continue with the work.

At the end of the year the overseers had to submit accounts of all payments and receipts to the vestry meeting in the parish church at Easter. If they had spent more than the meeting judged right they were expected to make up the difference from their own pockets. Cordell and Morton were pleased that their year was over and that their accounts had been accepted. It had been an easier year for them as the rate was lower than usual. Most of the money was raised by a rate paid quarterly but extra might come from the sale of goods of a defaulter. Widow Johnson's goods raised over one pound in this way in 1718. Other small sums came from the spinning done by paupers.

Jeremiah had arranged to take a gift of food to Susan Dickenson the local midwife who was unwell. Just before nine o'clock they walked to the parish church. They passed Bible close which had been bought with the gift of £50 under Dr Wilde's will and crossed Cow Lane (now called Ramsey Road) towards the vicarage. They passed the cottage of Thomas Townsend. They could see that preparations were being made for the baptism of his daughter Elizabeth on the morrow.

The next day would also see the funeral of Ann the little daughter of John Knightley. Family and friends were gathering to view the child's body, dressed in white wool according to law. This was intended by the government to increase the wool trade. If they could afford it, her parents might have sent their clothes to be dyed black. The guests would be given tokens to commemorate her short life, perhaps black gloves for the family and white for everyone else. An alternative gift was a mourning ring with a piece of the child's hair inside it. As John Knightley was not a wealthy man he was offering bunches of rosemary as a gift of remembrance and a funeral biscuit. This was a sponge finger spiced with seeds as a symbol of resurrection and renewed life, wrapped in crepe paper edged in black. Tomorrow the procession would walk its sad way to the church led by the vicar in his long black gown, with an attendant called a mute with a rod draped in black. Mourners and attendants would accompany the little coffin and the church bell would toll three times for a child, six times for a woman or nine times for a man. Funerals were far more formal than weddings. The inventory of John Parnell, a wealthy man, who died in 1690 gives some idea of the expenses associated with a death and funeral. Sixpence was charged by Mr Rabey, the apothecary, for medicine called physick. Five shillings and sixpence was paid to the nurse. The cost of the coffin and clothes for the deceased came to one pound and four shillings. Funeral charges were another pound. There was an additional charge of six shillings and sixpence for taking the body to Huntingdon for burial. The total cost was £3 16s 8d.

Death was a constant companion in the eighteenth century and the average life expectancy was only thirty-seven years. Many children

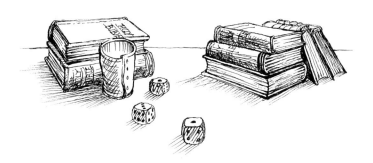

died in infancy. In 1724 Pettis tells us that *'the small pox all parts of the Town even from the priory to ye Green farm and dyd 75 persons of it from the 25 May to the 25 March following and 50 by comon sickness... inal 125.'* Devastating epidemics of typhus, dysentery, measles, small pox and influenza occurred with appalling frequency. Occasionally travellers passing through the town fell ill and died. They were hastily buried as in the case of Benjamin Manton, *'a stranger'*.

Jeremiah and his party entered the church and waited for the service to start. Under the terms of Dr Robert Wilde's will, six boys and six girls had already been chosen by the church and minister. They were *'of good report, all born in the parish, each above the age of twelve, and able to read in the Bible'*. Now they were present in church at nine o'clock in the morning to dice for the six Bibles. As the sermon bell pealed out, the minister and officers and 'other grave townsmen' stood around the altar with the twelve children. The minister prayed to God to direct the lots to his glory. A saucer with three dice stood on the altar. The first pair of boys each threw a dice and the one with the highest score won a Bible. When each pair of boys had thrown their dice the six girls did the same. The names of the six successful contestants were written in a book and then the names of the losers. If they survived until next Whitsun they could try again. Afterwards the six successful children sat together to listen to a sermon preached by the vicar in which he commended *'the excellency, perfection, divine authority etc of the Holy Scriptures. He pressed those persons to whom God at that day had given his word that they would be thankful and never sell, pawn or give away their Bible, whilst they shall have any more but one Bible.'* According to the terms of the will the vicar received ten shillings for his sermon and the clerk twelve pence.

The Puritan Dr Robert Wilde had been born in St Ives. He *'was a fat, jolly man, and a boon Presbyterus. But those who knew him most commended him, not only for his facetiousness, but also for his strict temperance and sobriety.'* He had a strong sense of humour. People used to tell one another examples of his wit. On one occasion he and another divine had preached as candidates for the living of Ayno. The Doctor being asked whether he or his competitor had gotten it, answered *'We have divided it. I have got the Ay and he has got the no.'* Yet *'he was excellently qualified unto his ministerial work; none more melted or melting in prayer, nor more serious and fervent in preaching Christ and His gospel.'*

When Dr Wilde died he left £50 to be invested in land which was expected to yield three pounds per annum. This became known as Bible close on the present site of the Health Authority clinic. In fact, the investment brought in three pounds and ten shillings. After the purchase of *'six plain and well bound bibles in English never exceeding the price of seven shillings for each'* and the payment of expenses, the remainder was to be used by *'the minister and churchwardens and such as they think good to invite.'* On this occasion Jeremiah had heard that there was to be a dinner in the comfort of the Crown Inn. After the service the party split up, Joseph's wife returning to the Unicorn along the lane north of the church called Poor Lane where she intended to make small gifts to some widows. Meanwhile the other three went off to visit John Cordell.

On their right as they walked up Cow Lane they passed Perly close which was a garden and orchard. Amongst the fruit trees and bushes they could see neat rows of vegetables to be sold in the market. Within the last century all the land between 'Audry Way' and the town had been taken out of the control of the manorial court and granted to individuals. Each small piece was fenced off with its own gate. Farmers benefited from the enclosed land because it was in one piece and they could farm as they wished. But others suffered a loss. As yet this was not a great problem in St Ives because only this part of the parish had been enclosed. But Jeremiah guessed that if all the land were enclosed, that is the three open fields, the meadow and the heath, there would be losers.

Those with only a few acres might find the cost of enclosing their land with a hedge and gate too expensive and might be forced to sell out. Those who did seasonal work, like weeding or harvesting, could at the moment supplement their earnings by trapping rabbits or collecting wood on the heath. They might graze geese and collect blackberries and nuts in season. But if the fields and the heath were enclosed and allocated to individuals their access would disappear and all these supplementary sources of income would dry up.

The closes were valuable properties and often owned by tradesmen, like bakers or innkeepers. It was a convenient place to keep a horse, essential for delivering goods in the surrounding area. The Peacocks, owners of Perly close, had moved to Ramsey and rented their land with the adjoining house. The annual rent was £8 for the close and £2 for the house. This rent was fairly expensive because the house was one of only forty-nine properties to have the right to pasture animals on the Heath. Another thirty-two people could do this because they owned arable land or meadow. All houses with common rights were in the western part of the town in the area known as Slepe. Mr Dingley Askham was gradually buying up these rights to increase the number of animals he could put on the Heath. He then received income by renting out the right. He was pulling down the old houses but keeping the right of common.

They were to visit John Cordell whose house was on the right at the top of Cow Lane at the crossroads. To their left they could see Green Farm owned by Sir Edward Lawrence. Behind this house was the old barn which townsmen called Cromwell's barn although Jeremiah had heard that it was built long before Oliver Cromwell. Edward Revell, a Quaker, lived next door. He was in frequent trouble for his refusal to pay rates for the repair of the church. In 1707 he had been charged '*to pay to Henry Underwood gentleman or to his Procter £1.3s for the case lay'd against him and alsoe 4/- for the fees and execution of his motion on and before the 16 of September – otherwise to appear at Huntingdon in the Parish Church of All Saints between the hours of 10 and 12 in the forenoone for non-payment thereof to see and heare himself excommunicated.*' Now he was having problems with the church again. He was one of sixteen people who owned arable land but only he and Jeremiah's friend Cordell were active farmers. The others rented their land to tenants. Between these farmhouses the road widened out and was marked by a large wooden cross. To the north was the road to Ramsey and Hust (Woodhurst and Old Hurst). To the east the cross pointed to Ely and to the west to Huntingdon. During the middle ages the fair of St Ives had extended as far as this cross which was similar to the one at the top of Bridge Street.

John Cordell's house had been badly damaged by lightning a few years earlier but it was now fully repaired. The brothers were welcomed into the parlour with its handsome cane chairs and tea tables. Although it was May a fire was burning on the hearth to make the room seem welcoming. John Cordell's appearance may have been that of a countryman pure and simple. He had the appearance of a '*common country farmer, a great coat with brass buttons, frock fashion, his hair short, strait, and to appearance uncombed, his face rough, vulgar and brown, as also his hands.*' Yet the two brothers knew that he was well educated and devoted to the service of the town. He was pleased to see his guests and quick to offer them tea. His wife performed the ritual of measuring the precious tea out of a canister from a lockable tea chest. At this time, tea was heavily taxed, making it the most expensive of all household commodities. Her little maid servant was only trusted to pour the water into the teapot. Sugar, coffee, confectionery and spices, were always locked away in the closet to prevent pilfering. Her teapot was made of porcelain and stood on a matching stand. Beside it stood a shallow cup with no handle on its own saucer. Sugar lumps were taken from a covered bowl with nips. Her guests were offered a piece of home-made gingerbread. The conversation quickly turned to John's complaints about his son-in-law. Their daughter Margret Mary had married Thomas White who owned the Mitre and coffee house in Bridge Street. John was threatening to remove her from his will but had been persuaded by his wife to leave her five shillings a week for her life "*it being my intention that her husband shall not receive or reap any profit.*"

After tea was taken, the men went into the farmyard leaving the ladies to talk. Ann was asked if she would like a tour of the house. Next to the parlour was the storeroom which contained a press for making cheese, as well as 48 fleeces of wool, stools and chairs. Her hostess was keen that the London visitor should realise that hers was a well-equipped house. She opened her chest of drawers and her wooden trunk with its domed lid to reveal all her linen, eight pairs of sheets, two board cloths for the table, many napkins and pillowbeers (pillowcases). Ann had already seen the teaspoons, tongs and strainer. Now she was asked to admire the punch ladle, porringer, watch and a pair of spurs kept in the chest of drawers. They looked into the brewhouse where beer for the family was brewed, and into the pantry where the beer was stored in barrels, with glass bottles and plates. The family ate in the kitchen at two tables seated on leather chairs. Here was a prized possession a coffee mill, a rarity in St Ives. In the buffett (sideboard) were stored the best sets of china plates, decanters, the family Bible and a reading glass. Upstairs were three bedrooms, the best chamber with the great bed with curtains, feather mattress, bolster, pillows, quilt and blankets. Off this room was the closet which contained household items not in regular use. Finally there was the second chamber with its bed, drawers, and four cane bottomed chairs.

Although Mrs Cordell was proud of her home and possessions, she was first of all a farmer's wife. As such she could *'fill the Muck-Cart, spread Dung and fodder cattle, drive a plough, handle a hedgehood and dress horses.'* She was an *'excellent hand at hedging and could stop a gap in a fence.'* Like most people in St Ives she enjoyed plain food and *'when they made a feast they had few French dishes; fricasees, oil's and rogouts were out of their way; and Gallimanfries and Galantines they did not know the meaning of.'*

Meanwhile the men were looking round the farmyard. There was a good barn and a stable converted from an old house. The granaries were raised on mushroom-shaped stone legs to prevent rats and mice climbing up. They saw his three carts, four ploughs and three harrows. There were riddles, sieves and screens for threshing. Harness for the six horses and mares was neatly stored beside saddles, forks, shovels and spades. Near the house, were two pigs, three cows and a calf whilst John told them that he had fifty five sheep and fifteen lambs in the field as well as his crops of wheat, barley, oats, beans and peas. Behind his farmyard were his five closes of twenty acres one of which was called Broad Leas.

He owned thirty-nine acres of arable land and rented another thirty. He also had fifteen acres of the meadow. Each autumn a parish meeting of farmers decided which crops were to be grown in the fields and which strips were to be left fallow. They rotated crops to prevent disease and also steeped seed in brine, lime, blood or urine as a further

precaution and they added lime to the soil to reduce its acidity. After land had lain fallow they liked to sow wheat or a pulse crop of peas or beans. Several cereal crops would be taken in succession, often with barley following wheat, and oats following barley, and then fallow.

At present Cordell was growing sixteen acres of wheat, three and a half acres of barley, the same of oats and beans planted together, and twenty-one acres of beans and peas. But as was the custom, his crops were scattered in strips (fifty-eight) across the three big fields. To show Jeremiah how his crops were doing they must walk the width of the parish from the boundary with Houghton to the road to Somersham.

The three men left the farm and walked along the road to Huntingdon until they came to Houton Field. On their left were the Hows of Sir Edward Lawrence and on the right the lower part of Ham Lang Field. At deadman's baulk they turned on to the track which had been used on May 16th Rogation Day when it was the custom for the inhabitants to beat the bounds. They took young boys with them so that they could learn the boundaries of the parish. At specific points the boys were beaten to assist their memories. It was also the custom for the vicar to bless the crops and people living in places along the route offered hospitality. Cordell told Jeremiah that this year the route had been changed to make sure that they traversed all the boundaries. *'The inhabitants went round all the bounds of the parish about with drum and colours.'* They started by taking a boat past the new staunch to the ditch which separated St Ives from Holywell fen. Here they met the second group. To cover the southern boundary the *'boat swam up to the brick kilns at the Hows'*. (This is now the bottom of the golf course.) The other company went round the edge of the meadow up past the closes to Stocks Bridge, on the road to March, along the eastern boundary. Then they went to the brick kilns to meet the boat and finally proceeded back by Houton field (the western and northern boundaries) to Stocks Bridge to complete the eastern boundary where the walk ended.

The three men walked past the first section of the field until they reached Ben Sheep where Cordell farmed six strips. They could see the sheep house in the corner. Sir Edward Lawrence owned the two fold-courses in St Ives. This meant that he had the exclusive right to erect a sheep-fold on the fallow from May to October. A fold was a temporary enclosure of wooden hurdles to keep sheep on the fallow areas. There was some advantage to the farmers in that his sheep manured their land. They next went to inspect his strips in Thorndown and Houghtonbrook. He wanted to see the women weeding these strips. It was backbreaking work and they needed supervising. In these strips he was growing winter wheat which he had sown last September.

Once the decisions about crops had been made in the autumn the horse drawn ploughs began to turn over the soil, burying the stubble and weeds. Ploughs were pulled by horses, sometimes four at a time. Cordell was fortunate in having six horses so that he could get his ploughing done with comparative ease. Poorer farmers worked together to get their land ploughed before winter set in. If the field had earlier been sown with an arable crop the land was ploughed four times. If it had been used as pasture or had lain fallow it was ploughed five or six times. They ploughed in straight ridges and furrows leaving several feet between the top of a ridge and the bottom of a furrow to help drainage. The furrows in a furlong lay in the same direction. One ridge and furrow formed a strip owned by an individual farmer. Several of these strips were grouped into furlongs or lands, each given its own name. All the fields were criss-crossed by paths and tracks and wet or boggy parts were left as grass. Cordell had two strips of indifferent land in Middle Water Land. After ploughing, farmers harrowed the soil to make a tilth for the seed. Seed was sown by broadcasting it, the labourer scattering it by hand from a

John Cordell's Strips

in the three common fields

Fields named are those in which Cordell owns strips, followed by the number of strips he owns over the total in that field.

· · · · · · · · · their route

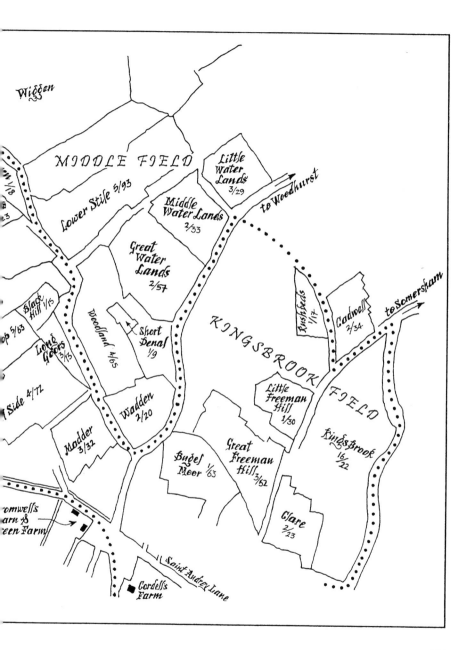

basket hung round his neck. It was then covered over by a second harrowing. For the next few months the main task was to protect the seed from weeds. This was labour intensive and depended on whether there were people to do the work and how much the farmer could afford to pay for their labour.

After inspecting the wheat they turned down the Ramsey road towards the Middle Field, parts of which were lying fallow this year to restore its fertility. On the northside of the Ramsey road were two very large fields called Wiggen Great and Little Field. Unlike the others they were fenced and full of grazing stock. They belonged to Mr Robert Piggott of the Priory and were not part of the common field system. Cordell would have been pleased if he could have his strips amalgamated into a whole. When they reached the fork they turned right into the Woodhurst Road to look at the strips in Mill Field, or Kingsbrook Field where there were more women weeding. They stopped to inspect the ditch on the edge of this field beside the road to March. In 1712 Thomas Houghton and Edmund Pettis had organised the cutting of the ditch and causeway along the line of the present Needingworth Road. Half the cost fell on the farmers of the neighbouring land like Cordell and half on the public as it was a public road. When the ditch was scoured the cost was shared with Needingworth.

In these strips he was growing spring crops. The land had been left untouched after the harvest to be broken up by winter frosts. The spring crops - barley, oats, peas and beans – had been sown between late February and April. They expected to harvest the crops in August and September with winter grains being cut first. Wheat and rye were reaped with a sickle, and barley and oats with a scythe. A scythe was too heavy for women but they were expected to help with stooking the grain. Once the crop was dry it was taken to the farm and stored until threshing. For a few days after the crops were cleared from the fields, women and children were allowed in to glean for loose grain. They collected it grain by grain and could take it home. Then the common herd was put on the fields until ploughing began again. The harvested grain was threshed as needed with a flail, a skilled task because it was necessary to separate the grain but not damage the straw. It was then winnowed by shaking it in a basket so that the wind blew away the chaff. It was finally sieved to remove the weed seeds and then bagged for milling or for sale.

The price of cereals was about ten per cent lower in the 1730's than in 1700. This meant that ordinary people were better nourished, although plenty of grain also meant more gin and therefore more alcoholism. But cheap food and high wage-rates depressed profits, and bumper yields meant a difficult time for farmers. Minor gentry and freeholders who were unable to diversify felt the pinch most. Many farmers went out of business, others got into debt, the lucky being hauled through bad times by far-sighted landlords. Rents fell into arrears or had to be reduced. Cordell was feeling some pain at the low prices but not to the same extent as other farmers. *'The small farmer is forced to be laborious to an extreme degree, he works harder and fares harder than the common labourer; and yet with all his labour and with all his fatiguing incessant exertions, seldom can he at all improve his condition or even with any degree of regularity pay his rent and preserve his present situation. He is confined to perpetual drudgery, which is the source of profound ignorance, the parent of obstinacy and blind perseverance in old modes and old practices, however absurd and pernicious.'*

In such families the work was shared between the men and women. Men did the hardest physical tasks – clearing land, ploughing, sowing seed, harvesting, and threshing – with the help of their sons or hired labourers. Women, helped by daughters or domestic servants, cooked, brewed ale, knitted, washed, taught young children, gardened, made butter and cheese, sewed, kept chickens, taking eggs, fruit, or vegetables to market, or doing some spinning or carding of wool. Women might help in the fields at harvest time, though their wages were about half to two-thirds of a man. They often did poorly paid tasks such as weeding. Small boys of four or five were paid to scare crows from the crops or to keep cows out of the corn.

As they followed the ditch past Great and Little Farthing Close they met with the town's pinder driving two cows. His job was unpaid and he had been unwilling to take it. It was his responsibility to collect any animals that had strayed into the growing crops and take them to the pound until the owner paid a fine and collected them. In this case he had found the cows in the hay crop and was now driving them to the communal pound. Cordell was relieved that they were not his cows. There was a second official called a hayward whose task was to decide

when the hay was to be cut and when animals could be put on to the meadow to graze. The hay was usually harvested in June and July. Grass was mown with a scythe and left to dry, raked into cocks and stored in a barn or rick. After the harvest the communal herd was allowed to roam all over the meadow until the spring of next year.

There were always tasks waiting to be done on a farm. Cordell did not have any woodland, but near the house there was a small orchard, kitchen garden, beehives for honey, pigeons for eating, ubiquitous pigs, geese, hens, and ducks. Hedges and ditches had to be maintained, buildings repaired, wood cut for fuel and, when he could afford it, women and children employed to remove stones from fields. As an arable farmer, his income came once a year when he sold his grain but he could sell his sheep at any time throughout the year. He kept breeding ewes for six years. As a dairy farmer, he had a steady income from milk, cheese and butter, supplemented by the sale of any male calves, barren cows and excess female calves which other farmers bought to fatten up for sale.

Time was now getting on and Jeremiah and Joseph said their farewells to John Cordell. They wanted to visit the old surveyor Edmund Pettis before returning to the Unicorn for a farewell meal. Pettis had come to St Ives in 1688. He had married Mary Taylour of Colne in 1691 and they had five children. To his great sorrow shortly after giving birth to her last child she and her new born daughter died. Ten years ago he had remarried another Mary. Joseph had told Jeremiah about the notebook and maps of St Ives made by Pettis. Townsmen had seen the old man walking around the parish drawing in his book. It was thought that the Duke of Manchester had commissioned Pettis to make a survey of his property. He had also helped to assess rents for the town so that payments for the land tax were fair. What he had to show Jeremiah was unique and fascinating.

Pettis had mapped the whole parish, showing the three big fields, the meadow, the closes and the centre of the town. On the maps of the agricultural areas he had drawn the strips into which the fields were divided and given the acreage and the name of the owner. Jeremiah could see that he had even drawn the footpaths, gates and trees. Pettis pointed out to Jeremiah how John Cordell's strips were scattered over the fields and meadow. But Jeremiah was particularly interested in the larger maps. One showed the whole parish, another the names and shapes of the different furlongs in the three fields, yet another all the land to the south of Audrey Way. The one he liked best covered the centre of the town. On this map in the centre of his book Pettis had drawn the frontages of the buildings with their windows, doors, chimney pots and stables. Jeremiah found this one fascinating especially when he found the Unicorn. He was sorry that it was not larger so that he could see even more detail. He did find that the handwriting was very small and he wished he could use Cordell's eyeglass to see more clearly.

As he turned the pages of the notebook he was surprised to see the amount of information that was included. He found lists of taxpayers with the amount of tax that everybody paid. There were lists of the houses which had rights to pasture animals on the Heath, the owners of all the closes with their annual rent, and full details of the land and houses owned by the richest people. Pettis had even worked out the total value of their investments. John Cordell's estate was valued at £72, but Mr Dingley Askham had more than £300. Sir Edward Lawrence had £376, and the Duke of Manchester £440. Jeremiah's own name appeared on the list of the taxpayers and he noted correctly that he had paid thirteen shillings and four pence in land tax. Pettis agreed with him how unfair it was that he had to pay an extra two pence in the pound because he was an outliver. This meant that he had to pay three shillings and four pence more. He had heard that it was not legal to demand this from outsiders.

Pettis was keen that Jeremiah should hear certain passages from his book. He was very proud of his part in the celebrations of the coronation of Queen Anne in 1702. He read out how he had formed the cavalcade in the courtyard of the church. It consisted of at least 238 persons, dressed to imitate the actual coronation. Nobody impersonated the Queen but they carried '*a table covered with a satan carpet embroider'd over, spread with damask on which was plac'd a crown adorn't with rings and jewels to a great value, also the scepter*'. '*Thus marshalled they marcht at true distance soberly gravily and as softly as foot could fall thro' the church yard, so descend down to the Sands and reach't allmost the length thereof. In the Bullock Market made a stand and the Prolocutor a speech, then a voly of small armes and a general Hue and Blessing the Queen, repeating it again at the Cross, in the Sheepmarket, the Waterside and Bridge Street, for so was their rout, wher a table was placed of 160 foot long at which the women and maddes were decently placed on each side (the youngest in quality march't foremost but the highest quality sett upermost), the canopy at the head.*

By this time an ox rosted whole was ready, cut out, dish't and serv'd up. After that 16 great cakes made for that purpose, the men atending them till they had dined. When they arose the men sat down. The women paid their respects in like maner. The streets, windows and balconies ware fill'd with spectators and they with satisfaction at so fine an asembly. And the good decorram keept no disorder happening tho several barrels of beer was set out to the popilas. The musick playing all the time of diner. The evening concluded with eluminations, ringing and bells.'

Pettis was interested in problems with the calendar. He told Jeremiah that he like others realised that '*Our calender wants regulating very much and tis a pitty the government don't take notice of 't for it might be brou't much nearer time.*' He knew some of the history of the calendar and read from his book passages about the changes made by '*July Caesar*' and Pope Gregory.

He wanted to show Jeremiah a drawing he had made of a compass. As a surveyor he was fascinated by such mechanical objects. He had also copied a complicated dial which showed the months, seconds, minutes, days, equinox (or as he said Equalnoction Line), and degrees of longitude. Within these circles were the names of places in the world and then the hour. Pettis showed Jeremiah that '*dialin to the meridian of London which is 12 or noon, Surat in East India is quarter past 6 aft'noon and at Mexico West India is three quarter past 5 in the morning and so according to which part of the world you are in.*' Another of his interests was the rising of the sun. '*We say suns rise as soon as we see it peep in our horrison but the astrominers don't count its riss tell the whole face of it be seen, which is four minuts from the first appearenc. So we say when the sun is quite out of seit its sett but then it is four minuts past as you see by its rising for 4 minuts from touching the horizon to its quite disaperanc.'*

He railed about problems with coinage. He thought that the King should call in all the gold coins and issue new ones. After all they both knew the coins of James I were worth 25 shillings, those of Charles I 23 shillings and some because they had been clipped or filed were only worth 17 shillings. It was all very confusing. He asked Jeremiah whether he had heard that *'all law writings, bonds, obligations, writts for arrest, copies from the Lords for estates'* were to be put in English next year instead of Latin. He thought this was a big improvement. Ordinary people would be able to understand what they were signing. Even as an educated man he could not read Latin. He had seen the records of the manorial court and knew that when Oliver Cromwell was the Lord Protector he had ordered legal documents to be written in English. When Charles I was crowned king this order was reversed. After so many years they could all rejoice at the change.

But Pettis like many Englishmen was vehemently hostile to Cromwell. Cromwell had farmed in St Ives. *'He farm'd hear tell he was very poor so that he let out some of his farme to two others.'* He had copied into his book some details of Cromwell's career but was much more interested in copying forged letters that proved that Cromwell had a bargain with the devil. Indeed he had reserved five times as much space for the account of this bargain with the devil as he did for Cromwell's career. *'It was in 1644 that Oliver receiv'd his commission from the Parlament and had another emediatly from the Devil and pleas'd both Masters which he knew was possible because they ware men and devils. This compact was made to answer his ambitious asspireing heart that so much thrist'd after honer tho to the loss of his soul.'* Vilification of Cromwell was common and Jeremiah was not surprised at such opinions.

By now it was getting late and they quickly returned to the Unicorn. As it was their last day his family had arranged a feast. The English delighted *'in feasting and making of good chear, eating much meat and of many sorts, prolonging their settings with musick and merriments and afterwards sporting themselves in set dances'.* All his

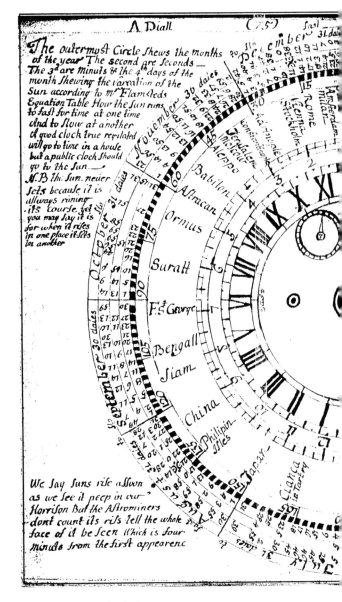

Pettis' drawing of a dial

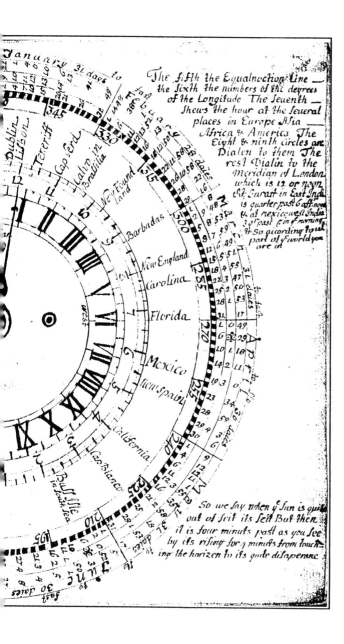

The fifth the Equalnoction Line the Sixth the numbers of the degrees of the Longitude The Seventh Shews the hour at the several places in Europe Asia Africa & America The Eight & ninth circles are Dialen to them The rest Dialin to the meridian of London which is 12 or noon the Surrat in East India is quarter past 6 after noon & at mexico west India 3 of past 6 in ye morning & So according to what part of ye world you are in

So we say when ye Sun is quit out of seit its seit But then it is four minuts past as you see by its rising for 4 minuts from touching the horizon to its quite disaperenc friends from St Ives were invited. They ate mutton marinated in blood and roasted on a spit before the open grate in the kitchen. The cook had also roasted some beef and a piece of pork garnished with cabbage, turnips and carrots swimming in a butter sauce. The term 'vegetables' was not yet in use. They were known as edible roots and herbs. The broth in which the roots were cooked was served as a thick soup. While this first course was being eaten smaller dishes were cooking. These included chickens and pheasants roasted with heads and legs intact, as well as duck and a goose prepared without the head. The large platters were placed in the centre of the table and people helped themselves. Nobody was expected to taste every dish. Drinks were served from the side-board. There was plenty of wine, punch and strong beer. Jeremiah and Ann as the honoured guests received the best portions. To accompany the second course, there was a sweet baked pudding with dried fruit and almonds in a puff pastry crust.

In polite society it was considered bad manners to *'baul out aloud for any thing you want; as, I would have some of that; I like not this; I hate onions; give me no pepper'* but I don't know whether folk in St Ives cared. To belch at the table was not considered any more unusual than to laugh or cough. Foreigners thought that the English ate to excess, drank like lords, and swore like troopers. Even fashionable ladies habitually swore. There was plenty of noise. Guests *'leapt to their feet to cheer and jeer. They laughed and cried out loud. They jested and capered, sang and shouted a lot; they threw themselves into the hurly-burly of fun-making, love-making, noise-making.'* Drinking was competitive. *'We continued drinking like horses, as the vulgar phrase is, and singing till many of us were very drunk, and thus we continued in this frantic manner, behaving more like mad people than they that profess the name of Christians.'*

Finally they staggered up to bed. The watchman had been asked to use his long stick to knock at the window to wake them early in the morning. They would get no more than a hour or so of sleep because the waggon left for London at dawn. They were on their way back to *"the chiefest emporium, or town of trade in the world; the largest and most populous, the fairest and most opulent in all Europe, perhaps the whole world."*

SOURCES CONSULTED

Bodleian Library, Oxford, St Ives Post Boy, 28.4.1718
Cambridge University Library, 'Dr Dale's visits to Cambridge 1722-1738'
County Record Office, Cambridge, Quaker records RG 6/1309, R 59/25/3/1
County Record Office, Huntingdon, Registers and Vestry Books, All Saints Parish Church St Ives; Manorial Records of St Ives; Inventories and wills; Registers of the Free Church St Ives;
apprentice indentures; Royston to Wansford Bridge Trust, copy of the amendment act, 1717; 'Biggleswade to Alconbury Trust', (A1 part), typescript copy of minutes 1725-1745; 'St Neots Scrapbook', 2-9 March, 1725/6
Lincoln Record Office, 'Speculum Dioeceseos Lincolniensis sub episcopis Gul Wake et Ed Gibson, 1703-1723';
Norris Museum and Library, St Ives Edmund Pettis's Survey of St Ives, 1728; G S Green 'The Life of Mr John Van, a Clergyman's Son, of Woody in Hampshire', undated but probably mid 18th century
Public Record Office, SP10/7; E/126/12 FO. 22-23,26; War Office Survey of Beds and Stabling, 1686; ASSI 35/177/13; E134, 11/12 Chas 1 Hil 10

W Albert, The Turnpike Road System in England, 1972
R Bayne-Powell, Travellers in Eighteenth-Century England, 1951
P Brears, A Taste of History, 10,000 Years of Food in Britain, 1993
B Burn-Murdoch, The Pubs of St Ives, 1992
B Burn-Murdoch, St Ives Bridge and Chapel, 1988
J R Cox, An Illustrated Dictionary of Hairdressing and Wigmaking, 1989
P Cunnington, Care for Old Houses, 1991;
Jack Dady, Beyond Yesterday; A History of Fenstanton, 1987;
D Daiches & J Flower, 'Dr Johnson's London' in Literary Landscapes of the British Isles; A Narrative Atlas, 1979
D Davis, History of Shopping, 1966
D Defoe, A Tour through the Whole Island of Great Britain, (1724-6), ed P Rogers, 1971
T De Laune 'The Present State of London' 1681; 'The merchant and Trader's Necessary Companion', 1715
R Dodsley, The Art of Preaching, 1738
A T Hart, The Eighteenth Century Country Parson, 1955
C Hibbert, The English; A Social History 1066-1945, 1987
P Hughes, 'Some Civil Engineering Notes from 1699', in The Local Historian, 26, 2, 1996
S Inwood, A History of London, 1998
C McDowell, Hats; Status, Style and Glamour, 1997
E D Moore The Fairs of Medieval England, An Introductory Study, 1985
L Munby, How Much Is That Worth, 1996
H E Norris, History of St Ives, 1889, reprinted 1980
K Olsen, Daily Life in 18th Century England, 1999
R Porter, English Society in the Eighteenth Century, 1990
B Reay, Popular Cultures in England, 1550-1750, 1998
J Richardson, The Local Historian's Encyclopedia, 1977
F W Steer, Farm and cottage inventories of Mid-Essex 1635-1749, 1969
J Stevenson, Popular Disturbances in England, 1700-1832
C F Tebbutt, Extracts from Assize Rolls of Huntingdonshire in the Seventeenth Century
J Thirsk, ed, The Agrarian History of England and Wales, Agrarian Change 1640-1750, 1985;
G L Turner, Original Records of Early Nonconformity under Persecution and Indulgence, 1911
Victoria County History, Essex, vol 2, 1907
Victoria County History, Huntingdonshire, vol ii, 1932;
M Waller, 1700; Scenes from London life, 2000
S and B Webb, English Local Government: The Parish and the County
B Worden, Stuart England, 1986
A Young, A Six Weeks Tour through the Southern Counties of England and Wales, 1768